Praise for *Stones of Time*

"Oertel's dialogue is clever, his characters are attractive and convincing, and there is a good combination of historical information and fantasy."
Winnipeg Free Press

"Besides enjoying a fast-paced adventure story, young readers will learn about the solstice, time travel, and ancient Cree culture in this volume that easily stands on its own."
Kirkus Reviews

Praise for the Shenanigans Series

"A fun, engaging series for adventure and history buffs."
Quill & Quire

"A fabulously fun series that . . . will appeal to boys and girls alike."
The Literary Word

STONES of TIME

Wandering Fox Books
An imprint of Heritage House Publishing Company Ltd.
heritagehouse.ca

Cataloguing data available from Library and Archives Canada

ISBN 978-1-77203-058-7 (pbk.)
ISBN 978-1-77203-059-4 (html)
ISBN 978-1-77203-060-0 (epdf)

Series Editor: Lynn Duncan
Proofread by Lesley Cameron
Cover design by Jacqui Thomas
Interior design by Vivalogue Publishing (Canada) Ltd.

Cover photographs:
Liz Bryan
two boys—Jorgen McLeman/shutterstock.com
girl—Nowik Sylwia/shutterstock.com

This book was produced using FSC®-certified, acid-free paper, processed chlorine free
and printed with vegetable-based inks.

Heritage House acknowledges the financial support for its publishing program from
the Government of Canada through the Canada Book Fund (CBF), Canada Council
for the Arts, and the Province of British Columbia through the British Columbia Arts
Council and the Book Publishing Tax Credit.

 Canadian Heritage Patrimoine canadien BRITISH COLUMBIA ARTS COUNCIL

19 18 17 16 15 1 2 3 4 5

Printed in Canada

STONES *of* TIME

The Shenanigans Series—Book Two

ANDREAS OERTEL

WANDERING FOX

An imprint of
HERITAGE HOUSE PUBLISHING
Victoria | Vancouver | Calgary

Writing a story is a solitary task, but turning a
story into a great book requires a team.
And I have an awesome team.
My sincere thanks to everyone at Heritage House
Publishing and Wandering Fox Books,
especially Lynn Duncan, Kilmeny Jane Denny,
Leslie Kenny, Lara Kordic, and Jacqui Thomas.

For H. and W.
For everything.

"Once confined to fantasy and science fiction, time travel is now simply an engineering problem."
Michio Kaku, Theoritical Physicist

PROLOGUE

ANNA WAS COLD, and she was terrified.

A whole day had gone by since it had happened, though she still didn't know what had happened. She had been exploring a graveyard in Canada with her father when . . . when something went wrong. But what had gone wrong?

"Come on, Anna, think," she said to herself. She crouched into a ball under the forest canopy and tried to warm her bare legs by rubbing them.

Concentrate, Anna.

She recalled driving to the small town. What had the sign said? Welcome to Santana? Something like that anyway. Her father parked the rental car in a gravel lot adjacent to a sprawling cemetery. She remembered how excited her father had been as they left the car, heading off into the forested graveyard.

And then . . . then what?

She tried again to focus. Her last memory was of locating the "special" stones. Father was able to find them quickly because he'd been there before. He'd stumbled upon the ancient pillars weeks earlier, he explained, when he flew to Canada to investigate an ancient Egyptian tablet.

As the minutes passed, the fog lifted from Anna's brain and snippets of memory returned. She suddenly remembered helping her father measure the centre of the three-stone formation when . . .

A raven screamed somewhere in the distance, causing the goosebumps already growing on her arms to swell into little anthills. Anna bit her lip to fight back the tears.

Where am I?

She knew her father, the renowned German archaeologist, Dr. Bruno Wassler, had studied man-made rock formations for years. But she had never really listened to his theories about those petroforms. She just enjoyed being with her father, the famous— some said "crazy"—scientist.

Anna looked to the clearing where the three stones stood like sentinels. They certainly appeared to be similar to the ones she'd seen with her father in Canada, Egypt, and elsewhere, but she was definitely not in any of those countries now. She was somewhere else.

The stones were roughly chiselled to approximately four feet high, with a two-foot diameter base that tapered to a narrower top. These rocks were covered with moss and lichen too, but a lot less than the ones in the cemetery. Anna knew that if she examined their surfaces closely, she'd find hundreds of symbols and glyphs. The rocks, each ten paces from its neighbour, formed a triangle, and Anna had woken up in the middle of that triangle.

But why? And how?

The sun was beginning to climb above the treeline now, and she groaned with pleasure as it warmed her skin. It had been a long, cool night. This place felt like—and even smelled like—a normal summer morning in the Schwarzwald, the Black Forest, where she had grown up in Germany. But in her heart she knew she was someplace very different. How could she have been in a cemetery in Canada one minute, and then here in the next?

Anna now wished she had been more attentive to

her father and his lectures about these stones. What was it he was always telling Mama about? Cosmic markers? Solar calendars? Timelines touching? Quantum something? It had made no sense when he told her these things, and it still made no sense. But now she realized that perhaps she should have listened.

She felt guilty, because only yesterday on the drive from the airport to the cemetery, her father had seemed extra enthusiastic. "I have a new theory," he said, "that the symbols on the pillars are the key." But Anna was so excited to be on another adventure with her father, she never even bothered asking, "The key to what?"

How can I go home, if I don't even know where I am?

Feeling thirsty, Anna decided to walk back down to the river for a drink. She had discovered the river by accident when she first woke up and began wandering around, dazed and confused. The river was a five-minute walk to the east, and moving about seemed to help her think. Anna knew the turbid water would probably make her sick, but her mouth was so dry she didn't care.

Suddenly, something strange began to happen.

She looked around the clearing quickly, searching for whatever had alarmed her. The sun was now high overhead, and the pillars cast no shadow on the grassy ground. Everything seemed normal. But the hairs on the back of Anna's neck stood up, and she shuddered with trepidation. A low vibration began in the air above the stones and rapidly grew into a deafening thumping. She pressed her hands over her ears so hard, she thought she would crush her own head.

THUMP! THUMP! THUMP!

She squinted through the pain toward the petroforms in the distance. Anna desperately wanted to run away from the unbearable noise and those stupid stones—this had to have something to do with them. But she knew that whatever was going on now might be a clue to help her get back home.

So she stayed put.

The air over the stones continued to thump violently until it all ended with a final screech that sounded like the scrape of giant fingernails against a chalkboard. The abrupt silence and the relief from the painful pounding made a tear slide down Anna's cheek. She wiped it away with a shoulder and got up.

Wait!

There was a body lying in the clearing.

Anna hadn't seen the small shape in the centre of the pillars until she stood, but she was sure she wasn't imagining it. To be certain, she rubbed her eyes vigorously and focused again. Yes, there was someone there. That's exactly where I was when I landed here, Anna thought.

Her heart beat a mad rhythm as she approached the still form. Who could it be? Doesn't matter, she quickly told herself. At least she wouldn't be alone anymore. Perhaps, between the two of them, they could figure out a way back to the cemetery.

A raven—maybe the same one she had heard earlier—emitted a harsh shriek.

Anna froze twenty feet from the body. Was that a warning cry? She closed her eyes, alert to the sounds of the forest around her. She heard nothing, but then again, her ears were still ringing from all the thumping. But why was the raven screaming?

Anna moved forward cautiously. The body was that of a girl—a girl her age, perhaps twelve or thirteen. She was lying on her side with one arm under her blond ponytail.

Please don't be dead, Anna prayed.

The girl groaned and rolled onto her stomach.

KA-KAWWW! The raven shrieked again—louder this time.

Anna sensed someone might be approaching and felt a powerful urge to hide.

She knelt next to the girl's head. "Please wake up," she whispered urgently. She shook her gently and repeated the same thing in German. "*Bitte wach auf.*"

The stranger groaned, but her eyes stayed shut.

KA-KAWWW!

Panic rose in Anna. "We have to hide!" she warned.

She shook the girl again, and at the same time searched for cover. The girl opened her eyes. She smiled weakly and went back to sleep.

KA-KAWWW!

Anna hooked her elbows under the girl's arms and tried to drag her to the treeline. She made it five steps and collapsed, gasping for air. The girl's limp form was far too heavy for Anna to move alone.

The voice in her head implored her to run. *Go! Now!*

If she had more time, Anna could get them both to safety, but she didn't have a second to spare.

She had to hide *now*.

Anna left the girl amidst the stone markers and sprinted for a cluster of uprooted trees. Diving over a fallen spruce, she curled into a ball and rolled to a stop. She was in the mossy depression of a giant root pad left behind when wind had knocked over the entire tree. Anna was safe for now, though her feeling of security couldn't mask the regret she felt at having to leave the girl behind. She grabbed a fistful of damp moss and squeezed it tight, frustrated that she was too weak to save her.

Shouts reached her from the far side of the clearing.

Anna pressed her face into the damp earth and tried to still her breathing. She didn't think they had seen her, but she couldn't be sure.

She didn't dare look up.

Waves of broken speech reached her from the area near the pillars. The dialect and tone were unfamiliar to Anna. She was good at languages and fluent in German, English, and French, but she had heard nothing like this before.

Curiosity finally compelled her to chance a peek. A small gap between the fallen tree and the ground allowed Anna to see some of the area.

Eight men nervously formed a perimeter around the stones, while a ninth man examined the girl. A tree limb obscured most of his face, and he vanished from her sight quickly, but she saw that he had long hair and was at least a foot taller than his companions. The other men were clad in leathers and skins—they resembled the images of Native North Americans that she had seen in books.

Her heart raced impossibly fast. She had been so worried about where she was, she had never even considered *when* she was. These were definitely not people from her time. Had she somehow travelled to the past?

Anna had failed to listen to everything her father tried to pass on to her, but she wouldn't make that mistake again. She concentrated on every detail, searching for clues that might help her rescue the girl and get them both home again.

Five of the men held short bows and carried quivers on their backs with arrows. The other three were armed with fierce-looking spears. She examined the group and noticed they varied in age from older teenagers to senior citizens. The way the Natives were looking around and shifting about from foot to foot made Anna think they feared the stone formation.

Anna still couldn't see the tall man's face, but she saw him lift the unconscious girl and move her away from the petroform. Anna thought, from the way the man was holding the girl, he wouldn't hurt her. But she couldn't take that chance, so she remained hidden. And even though she longed for the company of humans, she knew the answer to returning home—to her own time—was here at the stones. She couldn't leave.

The pillars are the key. Her father had said so. If another girl from her time could find her way here, her father could too. I have to stay put—someone will find me. She had to believe that.

Anna's thoughts were interrupted when one of the shorter Natives began arguing with the tall man carrying the girl. Now what? She noticed that the shorter man wore a necklace with a peculiar assortment of teeth, claws, and bones dangling from it. He must be a band chief or tribal leader. The chief barked at the man holding the girl. Some of the others became impatient and gathered around the tall man, as if in support.

It looked like the chief wanted to leave the girl behind, but the taller man disagreed.

Finally, the tall man lowered the girl onto the grass and a stretcher was hastily rigged up using two of the longer spears and some pieces of leather.

As the party left the clearing, Anna whispered a quiet promise to the girl. "I won't abandon you a second time. I'll get you home too."

And there she waited, alone, as another cool evening replaced the warmth of the sun . . .

CHAPTER 1

"YOU'D THINK," ERIC griped, "the town would have a riding mower for a graveyard this big." He followed Rachel deeper into the wooded cemetery, dragging a push mower carelessly behind him.

"Maybe they do," I said, hauling a second mower after my friend. "But doing it this way is more like punishment. You know, the hard work of having to push a lawnmower and not just drive one around. That sort of thing."

Eric's mower snagged on a low gravestone. He stopped. "Yeah, I suppose you're right, Cody, because it would actually be fun cruising on a riding mower. Some even have drink holders for Slurpees—"

"Shhh!" I said, cutting him off. "Listen!"

"What is it?"

I held up my hand, signalling him to be quiet. "I

thought I heard a noise," I said ten seconds later. "Like . . . like . . . "

"Like what?" Eric asked.

"I was going to say lightning, but I guess that's kind of dumb." I pointed up at the cloudless sky.

Eric laughed. "Maybe it was Rach starting up the trimmer."

I shrugged and looked around for Rachel, Eric's sister. She had been pushing a wheelbarrow with extra gas and other gear, and I thought we were following her, but now I realized she was nowhere in sight.

Eric disrespectfully climbed onto a fallen headstone and surveyed the sprawling graveyard. "Where the heck did she go?"

"Well, yesterday," I said, "we stopped cutting grass when we got to The Funny Guy. So she's probably waiting for us around there."

Eric nodded and jumped to the ground. He jerked the lawn mower over the tombstone and worked his way west.

I followed him around the old headstones, heading deeper into the cemetery that had been our workplace for . . . for fifty-six hours. Or were we up to fifty-nine hours now?

It was hard to believe that only a few weeks ago we had fooled the world by planting a phony Egyptian artifact next to the river in our hometown, Sultana. Our goal had been a noble one. That is, if playing a hoax on the world so you won't have to move away can be considered noble. But our plan worked too well, and when the media frenzy grew out of our control, we began to feel guilty about what we'd done. So before anyone could arrest us and toss us in the Crowbar Hilton, we confessed to everything.

That's the reason we were now cutting the grass in the town graveyard. You see, you can't break the law, and confess to breaking the law, without consequences. That's the way a civilized society works. So our punishment for the crime of public mischief was performing one hundred hours of community service. And we spent most of those hours mowing the grass in the Sultana Cemetery.

It took almost two weeks before we stopped getting heebie-jeebies from all the tombstones. But now we were cool with the place. And we even had names for the different sections. We stored the extra gas cans near The Alphabet Guy, whose name seemed to use up all twenty-six letters. We took our breaks in The French Quarter, where all the French-sounding graves were clustered together under four towering oak trees. And we usually had lunch on The Funny Guy, because his grave was elevated and made a nice picnic table. I'm sure that's a bit morbid, but we didn't think the dead guy would mind. We were keeping him company, after all, and trying to keep the place looking nice for him and his neighbours.

Anyway, after five minutes of walking, we found Rachel, and sure enough, she was waiting for us where we predicted. Eric sat down on the headstone and read the inscription out loud.

CHESTER BASSANI

1899–1963

"I TOLD YOU I WAS SICK."

"That really is kind of funny," I said. "I mean, for a grave."

"Basically," Eric said, "what he was saying was, he died because no one believed him when he said he was sick."

"I'm pretty sure we get that," Rachel said.

Eric laughed. "I'll have to think of something funny to put on my grave too."

Rachel hoisted a gas can from the wheelbarrow and began topping up my mower. "How about something like this?" she said. "'My sister killed me, because I drove her crazy.'"

I nodded. "Hey, that's pretty good."

"Or," Eric said, "how about, 'Being dead is better than living with my sister.'"

Rachel can take a lot of teasing, but I decided to change the subject just to be safe. "Did you hear a weird ZAP noise?" I asked her. "A few minutes ago?"

Rachel twisted her mouth in thought. "No. But maybe it was that little car we saw in the parking lot. Maybe the motor backfired or something."

"Maybe," I said.

"That was a rental car," Eric added. "It had rental licence plates."

"I noticed that too," I said. "I wonder what it's doing out here. In Sultana."

"Could be stolen," Eric said. "Or used in a heist and then dumped."

"Jeepers!" Rachel said. "Why are you two so suspicious about everything?"

"We're not," Eric said defensively. "We're just mulling over logical possibilities."

"Well then, why not start with the most obvious?" she said. "It's probably someone who rented a car at the airport, and then drove out here to visit a relative's grave."

"I guess we were letting our imaginations run away," I admitted.

"More like sprint away," Rachel said.

"Then why," Eric asked, "didn't we see a single person on the walk in?"

"Maybe they're still in the car," Rachel said, "eating sandwiches, or looking at a road map, or—"

A sudden commotion behind a hedge of cedars made us all jump and spin around. A man staggered around the trees and ran up to us.

"She is gone!" he cried. "Just like that . . . gone!"

We looked at each other, not sure what to say to him. He was in his forties, I guessed, and wearing cargo pants and a short-sleeved shirt with lots of pockets. He spoke with an accent—maybe he was Swiss, or German, or from one of those Scandinavian countries.

He looked vaguely familiar, but since I didn't

know anyone who had an accent like that, I gave up thinking about it.

Rachel, obviously feeling bad for the man, said, "Yes, death can be very sudden. But we're very sorry for your loss, Mister."

The stranger squinted at Rachel, and then shook his head. "No, no, no. She is not dead."

"It's nice that you come out here," Eric said, waving his arm around the graveyard, "to keep her memory alive."

The man was clearly upset about his wife's death. I nodded solemnly. "You should always keep her alive in your heart." I think I read that on one of the newer granite memorials.

"No," he squeaked again. "My daughter. She vanished only a moment ago. I saw it happen. Please help me!"

"What?!" Eric said, alarmed. "You mean, like a bear took her or something?"

I nervously scanned the area for black bears. Usually we made enough racket to keep them away, but it was possible there was one in the area.

"Please come with me," he begged. "We are running out of time!"

He disappeared around the cedars again.

Rachel grabbed her backpack from the wheelbarrow and followed the stranger, leaving Eric and me little choice. And if there's one thing I don't like, it's not having a choice. I was about to protest to Eric, when he shrugged and began tailing his sister. Oh, well, I thought. Maybe we could spend a few minutes humouring the man.

When we reached the oldest part of the cemetery, on the very edge of the wilderness, the stranger stopped. "It happened here," he said.

I noticed an old army-style rucksack on the grass. Scattered next to it was a tape measure and a bunch of pencils.

"What happened here?" Eric asked.

"My daughter, Anna, vanished."

CHAPTER
2

"OKAY," RACHEL SAID, gently pulling the man down, forcing him to sit on a toppled gravestone. "Just take your time and tell us exactly what happened."

He had been frantic and mumbling nonsense for five minutes, so it was good that Rachel was taking charge. I pulled a bottle of water from her backpack, opened it and passed it to the mystery man. After eagerly sucking down half the bottle, he seemed to calm down a bit.

Eric, getting impatient, said, "So this is where Hannah disappeared, huh?"

"Anna," Rachel corrected.

"Soooo," I said, "you want us to help you look around for her?" I didn't like all the weirdness and mystery, and to be honest, I was starting to feel pretty anxious.

"My name is Dr. Wassler," he finally said. "I am an archaeologist from Germany." That didn't really answer any of the questions we'd just asked, but at least we knew his name.

Dr. Wassler stood up, looked at his watch, and walked over to an old granite gravestone. After taking a deep breath, he said, "Does this stone appear familiar to the three of you?"

We looked at each other, and then at the four-foot-high rock.

I took a deep breath, forcing myself to remain calm. "Nope," I said.

Eric shook his head.

"Sure," Rachel said, "there are two more. One's over there behind those Jack pines. And the other one is next to that poplar."

Eric and I looked where she was pointing.

"Go figure," Eric said. "I never noticed it before, but you're right. There are three graves with similar stones."

"They are not graves," Dr. Wassler said. "These stones are astronomical markers. Together they make up an ancient petroform."

Rachel looked at the moss-covered pillar, then

turned and said, "Sorry, Dr. Wassler, but what do these stones have to do with Anna's disappearance?"

"Yes, yes, I am getting to that," he said, glancing at his watch again. "And please call me Bruno. That is my first name."

Rachel told him her name, then pointed to us and introduced Eric and me.

"How can they not be graves?" Eric asked. "They sure look like old tombstones. And we are standing in a cemetery."

"They may look like memorials," Bruno said, "but they are not. They have been here for hundreds of years—perhaps thousands. Settlers to the area likely imagined they were gravestones, and over time this became a community cemetery. But these three stones are definitely not headstones."

"I guess that's kind of interesting," I said. Then, to keep him focused, I added, "But what does that have to do with your daughter's disappearance?"

Bruno took another deep breath. "I will show you, Cody. And thank you for listening. I know this will sound extraordinary at first." He waved us closer to the nearest pillar and pointed at a symbol carved into the stone, near the base. The moss that he (or his daughter) had peeled from the rock was heaped on the ground. "Do you see this glyph?" he asked.

We nodded at an odd pattern of shapes surrounded by a box. Rachel pulled her camera out and began taking pictures of the chiselled objects. She had received the camera for her birthday and had been snapping graveyard photos all week.

"These are Mayan calendar symbols," Bruno said. "And they can't be found anywhere else in Canada."

Rachel nodded.

I nodded.

"So why's that a big deal?" Eric asked.

"The big deal," Bruno said, "is that the Mayans lived in southern Mexico and northern Central America. They were never in Canada."

"Whoa!" That was me.

Bruno pulled an old toothbrush from one of his shirt pockets and led us over to the second stone. He scrubbed lichen from part of the rock. "And do you see this chiselled text?" He tapped the worn characters with the worn bristles. "These are Chinese symbols from the Han Dynasty—the second century B.C. The ancient Chinese have never travelled here either."

"What about these?" Eric yelled, pointing at some etchings on the third pillar. "These look almost like … like hieroglyphics?"

Bruno wandered over to Eric. Rachel and I followed.

"Ah, yes," Bruno said, "I was going to show you those." He poured water from his bottle onto the granite, which made the characters easier to see. "They are from Egypt. Around 1300 B.C."

I took a step back. My brain tried to process what he was saying, but it couldn't. Nothing he was showing us made any sense. And I felt torn. My worry-wart side wanted to run home to escape all this nonsense. But my curious side wanted to help Bruno find his daughter.

"These three stones," he continued, "have glyphs and text from a dozen different cultures—Incan, Mayan, Druid, Native American, Aztec, Khmer, Egyptian, and the list goes on. Yet nowhere in recorded history do we have evidence of these people ever being in Canada—except for the Native Americans, of course."

I took a few more deep, calming breaths.

"And," Bruno said, "I have found similar stones in France, Scotland, Egypt, Mexico, and Thailand."

"But what does any of that have to do with Anna running away?" Eric said.

"Wait a minute," I interrupted. "You mean there are stones just like this in other countries?" I pointed at the glyph-covered stone.

"Absolutely," Bruno said. "They may be fading or deteriorating at different rates—depending on the local climate, you understand—but each stone is covered with similar glyphs, symbols, and codes. Some messages are etched in a coating of mortar, some are chiselled or carved into the stone, and a few are even painted." Rachel leaned in to take more pictures.

"And some of the symbols," Bruno continued, "are dates that make reference to time periods before, or well after, that culture existed. Some of the Mayan dates, for example, overlap the dates referenced by the Chinese Han Dynasty. This should be impossible, because the Mayans existed one thousand years before that dynasty."

"But how can that even be?" Rachel asked. "How can the stones here in our graveyard be decorated by ancient people from so many faraway places?"

"Look," Eric said, "do you want us to help you search for her, or not?"

Bruno glanced up at the sky and then down at his wristwatch again.

"If all those petroforms are real," I said, "wouldn't this be a huge deal? Wouldn't all archaeologists be talking about it? I never heard about Egyptians coming to Sultana."

"Until we made it up," Eric added.

Rachel shot Eric a nasty look and told the archaeologist to continue with his explanation.

Bruno took a deep breath. "Scientists do know about the sites," he said. "But no one wants to talk about it, because no one wants to consider the most likely answer."

"Which is what?" I asked.

"Time travel," Bruno whispered.

"Okay," Eric said. "That's it. We better get back to work. It was nice chatting with you." He turned to go, and motioned for me to follow, but I was curious and wanted to hear more. Sure the whole time travel thing sounded nutty, but somebody must have left all those messages. Right?

"What do you mean about time travel?" Rachel said. I guess she was curious too. "What does that have to do with anything?"

"What do you know about atoms?" Bruno asked.

Eric groaned, like he thought Bruno was trying to change the subject again. Maybe he was.

Rachel, feeling more indulgent, decided to humour him. "They're super-small and they make up everything," she offered quickly.

Bruno nodded. "Very good, Rachel. And atoms are made up of many even smaller subatomic, or quantum, particles."

"Okay," I said.

"Okay," Rachel said.

"Whatever," said Eric.

"And," Bruno continued, "in laboratory studies, quantum particles are always appearing and disappearing."

"So?" Eric said.

"So where do they go?" Bruno asked.

"I don't know," Eric said, getting frustrated. "This is your story."

"Many physicists believe that the particles can— and do—travel back and forth in time."

"Okay . . . that's all very interesting," I said. "But I still don't see what any of that has to do with this petroform or with Anna disappearing."

"Yeah, we got work to do," Eric said. "Wrap up your story already."

As you can see, Eric and I were both on the same page. We needed to him to get to the point, so that we could get on with our day.

Bruno ignored us both and carried on with his lecture. "I have a theory that every once in a while—under the right conditions—the past bumps and touches and rubs against the present. And when the timeline of history is affected this way, something incredible happens."

"What's that?" Rachel said, still intrigued by his story.

"A window—sometimes called a wormhole—opens up that permits people to move back and forth along the timeline. Scientists have already moved quantum particles forward in time using laboratory equipment. And I believe ancient people time-travelled using these astronomical markers."

Eric shook his head. "Now you really lost me," he muttered.

"But how?" I asked, getting exasperated. "And what happened to Anna?"

"To put it simply," Bruno said, "she fell into a

wormhole. The same wormhole described and documented by the writings on these stones."

"Wow," Eric said. "So the bottom line is: you believe your daughter time-travelled from this cemetery? Today?"

Bruno nodded, drank the rest of his water and wiped his mouth with his wrist. "I think there is one timeline—one history—for everything that has ever happened here on earth. And I believe these pillars mark the exact location of wormholes that will take a person back to specific moments on that timeline."

"So you actually think these stones," Rachel kicked the nearest pillar, "will allow a person to go back in time to get Anna?"

"Yes," Bruno said.

Eric was speechless.

"There are other, more experimental methods I could try to use to go back and locate Anna on the timeline. But this is the easiest."

"Wait a minute." I said. "Are you saying there are other ways to time-travel?"

"Most certainly," Bruno said, "There are Thomas Cylinders, Duncan Tunnels, and even Denny Entanglements. Any of these technologies could be used to travel back in time, but we need to travel to a very specific point on an unimaginably long timeline. And we need to do it now."

"That just doesn't make any sense," Eric said.

"Yes, it does, Eric," Bruno fired back. "Why would I use relatively unreliable Denny Entanglements to get Anna when I can use this petroform?"

Eric stared. "No, I didn't mean the Denny thing. I mean, this is all crazy." He waved his arms around the cemetery, making sure he included Bruno.

Rachel glared at her brother again for being rude. "So you have no idea where in the past Anna landed?" she asked.

"Because the timeline of history goes all the way back to the Big Bang, she could be anywhere. She might be with the Egyptians. She might be in a jungle where there are no people. Or she may have travelled to some period in prehistory we can't even imagine."

"My guess is she's right here," Eric said pointing at the ground.

Bruno nodded. "Yes, it is certainly possible she arrived at this location in the past. Perhaps three hundred or three thousand years ago. But she could also be at any of the other petroform sites, anywhere in the world."

"No!" Eric said. "I mean, maybe she got lost in this graveyard and wandered back to the parking lot. Maybe she's sitting in your car right now. Probably reading a comic book and sipping a root beer. I assume that's your car back there?"

Bruno studied his watch again, but didn't say anything.

We stood silently in the sun, forming a circle around one of the stone markers. I sort of agreed with Eric, and didn't believe anything Bruno was telling us. I mean, sure it was kind of interesting, but it was just way too far-fetched. On the other hand . . . if what he was telling us was true . . . Anna was in big trouble.

Rachel finally broke the silence. "I hate to say it, but if she could be in any time and anywhere in the past, how do you expect to find her?"

"Luckily all those ancient cultures marked the pillars with glyphs and symbols. And those are the clues."

Bruno shook his head.

"Unfortunately, Anna vanished before I could tell

her their meaning. If she knew what I know now, she could even come back on her own."

"But how exactly did she disappear?" Rachel asked.

Bruno walked to the centre of the triangle formed by the three stones. "Anna was helping me measure the distance from pillar to pillar so that we could triangulate the exact centre of the petroform site. The last time I saw her she was standing here." He looked down at his hiking shoes and frowned. "After she vanished—"

"What do you mean by vanished?" I said, cutting him off.

"She was waiting for me to write down the geometric centre of the stone formation in my notebook, when suddenly she disappeared. There was a sharp electrical snapping sound, and Anna was gone."

Whoa! Could that have been the noise I heard earlier? Goosebumps suddenly appeared on my arms. This is bad. This is bad. This is bad.

"Riiiiiight," Eric said, "she just fell down into some wormhole and never returned."

Bruno walked back to where we were standing, sank to his knees and began rooting around in his rucksack.

"I think I've heard enough," Eric whispered to me. "This guy really is a bit loony. Let's go."

But my legs refused to move. All the ridiculous things Bruno told us suddenly seemed possible.

Rachel wandered over to the centre of the stones, where Bruno had stood seconds earlier.

"So you're saying she was just standing here one minute, doing nothing unusual," Rachel said, "and the next minute . . . "

"NOOOOO!" Bruno bellowed. He jumped up, turned around and dropped his notebook.

But it was too late.

There was a snap of static energy, and Rachel was gone. I couldn't believe it. When I saw it happen on TV or in the movies, I knew it wasn't real. But this time I witnessed it with my own eyes.

She had vanished.

CHAPTER 3

"WHAT HAVE YOU done?!" Eric screamed. "Where's my sister? Get her back now!"

Bruno looked stunned. He ignored Eric and started mumbling. "Oh no . . . oh no, no, no. This is a nightmare—terrible. Not again, not again, not again."

I yanked on his arm and said, "What just happened? How do we bring her back? Tell us what to do!"

Bruno was shaking pretty badly, but he seemed to recover enough to talk. "I . . . I was about to ask if one of you would fetch Anna, but now this . . . "

"Now what?!" Eric shouted.

"Rachel does not know the secret to return either. I was about to tell you, but it all happened so fast . . . " Bruno gave Eric a mournful look.

"She does not know about the astronomical event.

And now they are both gone . . . both trapped in the past."

"This is not happening," Eric muttered.

Bruno wiped his brow with his wrist. "The window will be closing soon, so we have little time to prepare."

"Why can't you just go and get them right now?" I asked.

"Yeah," Eric said. "We'll wait right here. Just go bring Rachel—and Anna—back."

"That is the problem," Bruno said. "I can never use the wormhole."

"What!?" Eric screamed.

"I believe I am too old."

"Sure, sure," Eric said. "You just don't want to get sucked back in time."

"No, that is not true," he said defensively. "And I will try to explain."

"You'd better," Eric said.

Bruno pointed at the nearest pillar. "There are two ideas that appear to be repeated often on the stones at this location."

"What ideas?" I said.

"The glyphs on these three stones indicate that during a certain meteor shower, the wormhole at this location, here in the cemetery, opens up. The meteor shower does not activate the portal, it has simply been used by the ancient people to mark the event."

"Like a calendar?" I said.

He nodded. "Most ancient cultures did not have accurate calendars like we have today. Instead they used the sun, the moon, the stars, and other celestial events to predict and keep track of important events."

Eric looked up at the blue sky. "But there's nothing happening up there."

"I assure you," Bruno said, "the Perseid meteor shower is happening right now. You just cannot see it because it is daytime."

"Hmmph," Eric grunted.

"The petroforms at sites in other countries describe different astronomical events—solstices, lunar eclipses, and so forth. However, as I said, I do not believe these events cause the wormholes to open. More likely, people used the events to identify specific dates when they could time-travel."

Eric grunted again.

"I imagine," Bruno went on, "that for those first unlucky time travellers, the experience must have been quite a shock."

"Tell me about it," Eric said.

So he did. "One minute you are tending to your goats in Egypt, or shaping bricks for the Great Wall in China, or picking berries here in the forest, and the next minute . . . you are somewhere else entirely. I suspect that as those disappearances increased, people began to notice patterns."

"Patterns?" I repeated.

"Yes." Bruno nodded. "If anyone was paying attention, they would have noticed that people only disappeared during certain cosmic events and only from specific locations. And I am sure that as time passed, they marked those locations with the stones, and then documented the astronomical events with their warnings or instructions on how to get home."

"So I guess you're saying," Eric said, "the petroforms are kind of like instructions for time travellers."

"Yes," Bruno hissed. "That is exactly what they are—they are instructions for time travellers."

"What's the other idea?" I asked. "You said there were two things the other cultures wrote about."

Bruno nodded. "Many of the inscriptions mention youth, children, adolescence, innocence, and so forth. This seems to suggest that only young people

can use the wormholes. I am not sure why that is . . . "
His voice trailed off and he stared at the sky again.

I said, "I guess that explains why you didn't vanish
when you stood in the centre."

He nodded. "I would gladly go and bring the girls
back. This is entirely my fault and you . . . you should
have never become involved."

"Supposing that's all true," Eric said. "What do
we do now?"

"We shall quickly gather some basic supplies for
you both," Bruno said, focusing on the problem
again. "And then you can travel to the past, where
Anna and Rachel are. Find them, bring them back
to the markers where you arrived, and wait for the
proper astronomical event in that time and place.
Then the four of you can come back—safe and sound."

"What if we miss the event?" I asked. "What if it's
already happened where the girls are?" I didn't want
to be a pessimist, but he was making it all sound
way too simple.

Bruno looked at the spot where the girls had disappeared. "It is possible," he admitted. "But we have
to start with the most likely solution—that if you
hurry, you will arrive at a portal that is linked to

this wormhole. And that wormhole should remain traversable as—"

"Tra-what?" Eric said, cutting him off. "What does that mean?"

"Sorry," Bruno said. "That means the wormhole can be travelled: forward in time, and backward in time."

"This is one hundred percent nuts," Eric said. "But I guess we don't really have a choice," he finished, quietly.

"Do you think we should call your mom," I asked, "or my parents? You know, let them know what's going on?"

"No way!" Eric shot back. "My mom will go totally bonkers."

"But she might be able to help—call the police, or the army, or some weird agency with black SUVs."

A half hour had now passed since Rachel disappeared, and we were at Eric's house, rummaging for the supplies we might need on the other side of the wormhole. We all agreed that we couldn't just appear—wherever we might appear—with nothing.

We needed stuff. So we raced through the house, frantically shoving extra clothes into our backpacks. Bruno reminded us that we might all appear in a cold climate. Great, just great.

"I hope the girls are about the same size," Eric said, hustling downstairs and heading for the kitchen.

"Yeah," I mumbled, slightly distracted, "me too."

You see, I was obsessing over ten things at the same time, and to tell you the truth, worrying about whether or not a sweater fit Anna was at the bottom of the list. I thought I had all my irrational paranoia and improbable fears under control, and now I found myself facing the ultimate unknown—travelling back in time. Through a wormhole! Unbelievable. I shook my head at the unfairness of the situation.

Eric dumped another eight-pack of granola bars into his backpack. "Why are you shaking your head?" he asked.

"Huh?" I said, and then quickly added, "Oh, nothing."

You have to understand, for a Worry McWorry-Pants like me, this situation was a major nightmare coming true. An hour from now, I might actually find myself in a nest with a T. Rex. Or in a volcano. Or on a glacier. Or—

"Cody!?" Eric said.

I snapped out of it. "Sorry. I was just . . ."

"I know, I know. You were freaking out," Eric said, now shovelling drink boxes into his backpack. "That's obvious. But we have to stay focused. We have to keep it together for Rachel's and Anna's sakes."

I nodded, watching as Eric looted the refrigerator. Maybe, when he said we had to stay focused, he meant we had to focus on taking enough food with us to last until Halloween.

"I'd better find a cooler," he said, "and maybe some ice packs."

"What!?" I said, staring at the giant salami Eric was holding.

"All these cold cuts. They'll go bad if we don't keep them cool."

"Forget the meat," I said, trying to zip up my backpack. "We have enough food. And besides, we can't carry any more stuff."

After reluctantly putting the salami back, Eric closed the fridge. "I suppose we're ready then."

"Check the paper one more time."

Eric scanned the list Bruno made for us. "Yup," he said, "that's about it."

We left the house and jogged (waddled, actually) back through the woods. When we neared the cemetery, I stopped to catch my breath. "You sure you don't want to tell your mom what's going on?" I asked again.

"There's nothing," he huffed, "that she could do . . . that will help Rachel or Anna. We have to sort this out on our own."

I agreed with him, and it was a relief to hear him say what I'd been thinking. There really was no way anyone would believe what we had seen today. If we called the police, all three of us would be taken away and questioned for days and days. No one would ever accept that Anna and Rachel had just vanished into thin air—that's crazy talk. And if we didn't get back to those stones quickly, and through the wormhole fast, it would be too late for the girls—maybe forever.

How did we get into these situations?

Back at the petroforms, we found Bruno pacing circles around the centre of the stones. When he heard us approach, he jogged over. "You have everything?" he asked.

"Almost," I said.

"Yeah," Eric said. "We need a satellite phone. One that will work from anywhere on earth."

Bruno frowned. "That will not help you in the past."

"We know that," I said. "But what about when we return? What if we come back through the stones in Cambodia, or on a mountaintop in Peru? Don't you think we should call you when we get back with Anna and Rachel?"

"*Mein Gott!* My God!" he said. "I never even considered that. But . . . but there is no time to purchase a satellite phone." He pulled a smart phone from his cargo pants and gave it to me.

"But how can we contact you," I asked, "if we take your phone?"

Bruno frowned. "I will wait right here for you in this cemetery. But should a complication arise on your return, and you find yourselves somewhere else, telephone anyone."

"Anyone?" Eric said.

"Yes," he said. "Phone your parents. Phone the police. Phone anyone you can. Be as resourceful and creative as you need to be. Like when you made that tablet and . . ." his voice trailed off.

"I knew you looked familiar," I said. "You were at the press conference."

Bruno nodded slowly. "That is true. I flew here a few weeks ago to investigate the authenticity of the Sultana Tablet. And I recognized you this morning when I . . . when I was looking for help."

"And you knew we made that fake plaque?" Eric asked.

"Yes, yes," Bruno admitted. "That was actually the coincidence that helped me find these stones."

"You're going to have to explain that one," Eric said.

"I'll try," Bruno said. "But you should both get into position first. The Perseid meteor shower occurs for three days, and it comes in bursts. I don't know if the time portal reacts the same way, but you may as well catch the next opening of the wormhole."

We put on our backpacks and walked to the centre of the three-stone formation. He made us stand back-to-back in the spot where Rachel vanished.

He continued. "After hearing reports that an ancient Egyptian tablet had been discovered in the area, I had to investigate. You see, if a real Egyptian plaque was actually unearthed in Sultana, it would have confirmed my theory of a time-travel portal.

Anyway, while the other experts were evaluating the tablet, I was exploring the area for wormhole markers. And I was not disappointed. The petroforms were right here in the cemetery. I was ecstatic."

"So you suspected there might be pillars in North America," I said, "but it wasn't until you heard about an Egyptian tablet being found in Manitoba that you located them?"

"Correct," Bruno said. He gave us a sheepish grin. "I knew that the Native North American symbols on the pillars in other countries resembled glyphs found in cave art in central Canada—Manitoba, to be precise. So I estimated, or guessed, that there might also be similar stones somewhere in Manitoba."

"So our fake tablet actually got us in trouble twice," Eric observed.

Bruno seemed not to hear Eric. "One of my earlier theories involved the use of dark matter to open the portal and allow time travel along the timeline. I thought that if your plaque was real, I could analyze and test it in the lab. But of course, that theory is crazy."

"Not like everything else," Eric mumbled.

"Pardon me?" Bruno said.

"Nothing."

After a half hour passed (without us being sucked into a wormhole), we both got tired of standing and sat down on the grass. Bruno had stopped pacing and was now searching in his rucksack for something.

"Anything else we should know?" Eric asked. "You don't seem to want to tell us anything unless we ask."

"Hmmm?" he mumbled absently. Then, a few seconds later he cried, "Aha, found it!" He tossed me a walkie-talkie and stepped back again.

I waited for him to give me its twin, but he didn't. "This isn't any good," I said, "unless you can find the other one."

Bruno either didn't understand me, or he just felt like replying in his own roundabout way. "Anna," he began, "likes to explore the archaeological sites I take her to on her own, so we use these portable two-way radios to stay in touch."

Eric and I waited.

"They have a range of about one kilometre," he continued. "I am sure she has the other one in her pocket. Mine was not turned on, because she had not wandered off. If she had left the area, we would have stayed in touch with the walkie-talkies."

I clicked on the radio, pushed the talk button and said, "Hello. Can you hear me, Anna?" I don't think any of us expected a response, but we all held our breath anyway. I waited a full minute and then turned the power off again.

"If Anna switches on her radio," Bruno said, "you might be able to speak to each other, and to find each other."

I jammed the device into one of the outer pockets of my backpack and settled in to wait some more.

Five minutes passed before anyone spoke again.

"This is a horrible day," Bruno said with a sigh, "but it is also a momentous day."

I wanted to say, "More horrible than momentous," so I did.

He ignored that (as I expected) and continued. "You four young people will be the first people in modern times to travel back and forth in time. And you will be doing so using the instructions left by ancient people on these petroforms. I always suspected this was the purpose of the stones, and now I have proof. You are the proof of my life's work."

I had no interest in being the person who confirmed his crack-pot theory, but I kept my mouth shut.

"In the movies," Eric said, "when people time-travel, bad things often happen."

Bruno's gaze shifted back to us. "I am sorry?"

"Well," Eric explained, "when people from the future (namely us) interact with people from the past, doesn't that create problems? I mean, what if we make a bunch of cavemen sick with our germs? And what if they all get sick and die because of us?"

Bruno's face suddenly turned white. "You are absolutely right. Any interaction with the past, with any ancient civilization, could have devastating consequences. For the past, for the present, and for the future. You should just find the girls and come back. Do not linger."

My mouth was too dry to say anything, so I didn't even try.

Eric licked his lips, swallowed hard and croaked, "Okay."

"While you are gone," Bruno said, "I will try to think of a way to present my discovery to the world."

"I think it may be starting!" Eric yelled suddenly.

"And be very careful," Bruno warned. "If you can time-travel—"

"Yeah!" I shouted. "I feel something happening too!"

We both jumped up.

I wanted to run from the stones as fast as my legs could carry me, but I knew I had to stay put—for Rachel's sake and for Anna's sake.

"What were you trying to say?" I asked Bruno. "Tell us quickly!"

Bruno took two steps back and yelled, "Beware of . . . other time travellers—"

And that was when we both fell into the wormhole.

I heard a loud bang of static electricity, and that was followed immediately by a sensation of falling. At first it felt like I was being sucked into some kind of waterspout, or tornado, or giant vacuum. After that, I just fell, but I didn't fall like I was being pulled by something—I fell slowly and endlessly. The whole thing could have lasted a few seconds, or it may have taken a month. Time had lost all meaning.

Then I felt a subtle change—a new sensation, like something was whizzing past as I fell. Could these be points in time, on the unimaginably long timeline of history?

I began to panic.

What if we ended up in different places? What if I fell onto an island full of cannibals? What if Eric landed in Australia? What if we never saw each other, or Rachel, ever again? And that was when I really started to freak out.

So I did the only thing I could think of to make myself feel better—I screamed my face off.

"AHHHHH!"

CHAPTER 4

"WAKE UP," A VOICE begged. "Please, they will come back soon." The voice belonged to a girl—a girl who spoke with a German accent. Just like her father.

Anna!

I ignored her and tried to return to the peace and quiet of my unconsciousness.

"Hurry!" the same voice said, getting more urgent. "We must leave this place now." I felt someone pulling my arm and then—

SLAP!

Ouch! That stung. I opened my eyes and saw a girl with short brown hair and big brown eyes kneeling in front of me. "You must be Anna," I said, rubbing my cheek.

Her shoulders slumped. "Yes, yes," she said, sounding relieved. "Did Papa send you?"

"Yeah." I felt too dizzy to stand, but I sat up and looked around the clearing for Eric. Only he wasn't there. "Oh no!" I groaned. Where the heck did he end up?

"Do not worry," Anna said. "Your friend is over there, throwing up." Anna pointed to a cluster of pine trees on the edge of the clearing. I noticed her arm was scratched up and covered with bug bites.

"That's great," I said. "I mean, not that he's sick, but that he's here."

Anna realized she was still pulling on my arm and let go of it. "We have to leave this place before they return."

Eric wobbled over on shaky legs. "I feel awful," he moaned. "But am I ever happy you're here with me."

I tried to stand up too. "Yeah, and Bruno was right about everything so far. We landed in the same place on the timeline as Anna. Now we just have to find Rachel and get back home from . . . from wherever we are now."

"I think they took her away," Anna said.

"What?" Eric asked.

"The girl. Rachel. Is she about my age with a blond ponytail?" Anna asked.

Eric and I stared at each other.

"Yeah, that's her exactly," I said. "Have you seen her?"

"Yes," Anna said. She hesitated for a moment, looking almost guilty, like it was her fault Rachel wasn't with us now. "But as I said, they took her away," she repeated.

"Who took her?" Eric demanded.

"I do not know who they are." Anna looked nervously toward the west. "But we must hide. Please. They will come for you both soon. Your arrival through the stones made a lot of noise."

She was making me feel very edgy now. I scanned the forest around us for signs of danger. There didn't seem to be anything alarming, but Anna's fear was contagious.

"Okay," I said, picking up a backpack. "Show us where to go."

Eric snatched up the other bag and we followed Anna on our still-rubbery legs toward the east. It should have been an easy hike through open forest, but my chest felt unbearably tight. I suppose travelling through time can be hard on the body.

Anna stopped every few hundred feet so that Eric

and I could catch our breath. I took the time to look around. Something niggled at the back of my mind—this place seemed so familiar, like I had been here before. I shook my head. Maybe time-travelling was hard on the brain too.

After about fifteen minutes, we came to a river and took a longer break. I opened one of the backpacks and distributed some granola bars. We watched as Anna eagerly devoured hers. Since Eric and I were still feeling woozy, we passed her our ration.

And since I'm on the subject of feeling woozy, I think my brain really wasn't working properly. Something Anna was telling me did not compute with what I was experiencing. But I couldn't quite put my finger on it . . . yet.

"Thank you," she said.

I gave her a water bottle and waited for her to wash down the heavy bars. Eric walked over to the river bank and splashed his face.

I turned to Anna and introduced myself—in all the rush, we hadn't had a chance. "I'm Cody Lint, and that's my best friend, Eric Summers. The girl you saw—Rachel—is Eric's sister."

"I'm so sorry. I tried to save her . . . but—"

Eric returned from the river. "It's okay," he said. "Just tell us what the heck's going on around here."

Anna explained in detail what had happened to her since she vanished from the cemetery. Fighting to control her emotions, she ended her story by describing how she had tried to wake Rachel, but couldn't before they took her.

"You did the right thing," I said. "There's no point in you both being captured."

"Yeah," Eric agreed. "If you weren't there at the stones today, we'd have no idea what happened to you and Rachel. We wouldn't even know if we were in the same time."

"What did these guys look like—the people who grabbed Rachel?" I really wanted to know if we were dealing with cavemen, or cowboys, or can—

"Did they look like cannibals?" Eric asked. I guess we were both thinking the same thing.

Anna raised her eyebrows at Eric. "No, no," she said. "They were nothing like that. They appeared to be North American Natives. In German we still say 'Indians.'"

"Are you sure?" I asked, though I was relieved to know we wouldn't be clubbed by cavemen.

"Yes, I am certain. My father is an archaeologist—as you know by now—and every summer I travel with him to explore petroform sites. Anyway, we have many books at home on Native North Americans."

"And that's what the people who took Rachel looked like?" I asked.

"Yes," Anna nodded. "They look just like the pictures in the textbooks."

Eric smacked a horsefly trying to bite the damp skin on the back of his neck. "What were they wearing?" he asked.

"They had straight black hair," she said. "All their clothing looked like it was made of animal hides and furs. I did not see any type of cloth. And they wore moccasins on their feet."

"Did they have huge headdresses on their heads?" Eric asked, rubbing the welt from the horsefly bite. "And were their faces painted with war paint?"

Anna looked back and forth between Eric and me. Maybe she thought Eric was teasing her. "I think that is only in Hollywood movies. They seemed . . . peaceful."

"Good," Eric said, "because we've got enough problems already."

Anna tried to swat some black flies that were biting her already chewed-up ankles, but they were too fast.

I rummaged through my pack for insect repellent and passed it to her. "Thank you," she said. She squirted a big white blob on her hand and rubbed it all over her legs, arms, and face.

Meanwhile, I found Bruno's cell phone and confirmed what I suspected. The message on the screen flashed, NO SIGNAL FOUND. And how could it? There wouldn't be cell towers for who-knew-how-long.

"That's too bad," I said, returning the phone to the backpack. "It would have been nice to call Anna's dad to tell him we're just down the road."

"That's for sure," Eric said. "But at least we know we're in North America—in a boreal forest. And we have a river right here, just like in—"

"That's it!" I cried.

"Huh?" Eric said.

I had been looking up and down the river, wondering why the walk from the stones seemed familiar. And then it hit me. "Guys—I know exactly where we are."

"What is it?" Anna said.

"This has to be Sultana—from five or six or seven hundred years ago, but still the place where our future Sultana will be. We could have ended up at any of the other petroform sites on earth, but we didn't. We got lucky and landed at the same spot, only in the past."

Eric didn't look convinced. "Just because there's a river down there doesn't mean this is Sultana."

"No," I said, "look around, Eric. Think about it. In our time, it takes about ten minutes to walk from the graveyard to the river. Right?"

Eric nodded. "Yeah . . ."

"Well, that distance is exactly the same as what we walked from the pillars here, to the river. That can't be a coincidence. I think we're looking at the Kilmeny River—our Kilmeny River."

"I don't know . . ." Eric said, sounding doubtful. "Wouldn't all the glaciers during the ice age have changed everything?"

"Well, yeah," I said, "but that's way before now. Remember what Miss Kelly told us in school? Geologically speaking, five hundred years, or even a thousand years, is like the blink of an eye. It's no time at all in the Canadian boreal forest."

Eric waved his arms through the air. "But what about the trees? They don't look the same."

"Sure, the trees look different—there will probably be a hundred forest fires here in the future—but the rock outcrops, and the shape of the river, and the features of the land are the same."

Eric stood up and re-examined our surroundings. I watched as he took everything in, and then slowly began nodding. "Holy smokes! I think you're right. I think that granite outcrop way back there is where they'll put the west end of the bridge years from now."

"I can't be a hundred percent sure," I said, looking at Anna, "but if that's the Kilmeny River, the Red River will be just around the corner. And if we walk west for a day or two, we should find the start of the prairie—the Great Plains. We're probably here long before any Europeans, but I think this is the forest around Sultana, Manitoba."

Anna nodded. "I was only in your Sultana for a few hours, but I believe you are right."

"This could also help us find Rachel," Eric said. "All the houses and streets are missing, but we know this area like the back of our hands."

"Well, we used to, anyway," I said. "I'm sure all our

favourite trails and shortcuts are gone, but yeah, the area is the same."

"So far," Eric said, "Anna's dad was right about all the time-travel stuff. And if our luck holds, we shouldn't have trouble getting back."

Anna's eyes widened. "What did Papa tell you?"

I remembered that Anna had no idea what had happened to her, so I filled her in. "Your dad figured out that the pillars mark the spots where wormholes are located on earth. And ancient people used astronomical events to record when those wormholes opened so they could travel back and forth in time—along the timeline."

Anna was quick. Right away, she asked, "Then why did Papa not come and get me?"

"For some reason," Eric said, "only young people can time-travel, and only during certain gastronomical events—"

Anna blinked. "You mean astronomical?"

"Huh? Yeah, whatever," Eric continued. "Anyway, the meteor shower taking place right now back home marks the opening of the wormhole portal."

"Let us hope," Anna said, "that same meteor shower is still occurring here."

"Your dad was telling us what happened to you," I said to Anna, "when Rachel accidentally fell into the wormhole too. We didn't really believe him until we saw her disappear."

"I am sorry," Anna said, "that you had to come here and rescue me—rescue us."

"No problem," Eric said.

"If your dad is right," I said, "the wormhole will stay open for another two days. That means we have forty-eight hours to find Rachel and get back to the stones where you found us."

"They will be searching for us too," Anna said, nervously looking at the dark forest. She explained that when someone comes through the wormhole, it makes an unbelievably loud noise. "They know that I am here somewhere, and now they know you are here. For two days I have been hiding and trying to avoid the scouting parties that move through the area."

"Wait a minute!" I shook my head and tried to focus. "Did you just say you've been hiding for two days?"

"Whoa!" Eric said. "That can't be right."

"I knew something didn't make sense," I said.

"All your bug bites, the way you look, how hungry you are—"

Anna's lip began to quiver. "You . . . you would be hungry too if . . ."

"No," I said quickly, "that's not what I meant. We followed you through the stones—through the wormhole—two hours after you disappeared."

"And one hour after Rachel vanished," Eric added.

She blinked away some tears. "But I've been here for days."

"We believe you," Eric said.

"You obviously landed at an earlier point on the timeline," I said.

"Papa always says that the quantum world is unbelievably strange."

"But how did you survive for so long?" Eric asked, looking at the forest behind us. Like me, he was probably wondering how she could've survived on her own without any trouble. "Weren't you terrified?"

"Many of the archaeological sites I go to with my father are in remote locations. We often stay in tents and spend weeks outside—like camping. I was frightened because of how I got here, but I am not frightened by a forest."

"Where did you hide?" I asked.

"And what did you eat?" Eric said. I rolled my eyes at him (of course, he would ask that) and he shrugged.

"During the day—when I felt it was safe—I ate only wild strawberries. They are small but there are many of them. And at night I made a bed of branches from the cedar tree and covered myself with even more branches. The Natives have not found me—but I think they know I am here."

"I wonder what they want from you," I asked. "Or with any of us, for that matter."

"I do not think they mean any harm," Anna said. "Maybe they only want to protect us from danger— from the wild animals. But we cannot be sure. I just want to go home."

You've got that right, I thought.

"Have you seen any wildlife?" Eric asked.

Anna nodded. "Oh, yes. I have seen many deer already—they are everywhere. And early this morning, when I climbed a tree to see the area better, I saw a family of foxes."

"But no bears?" Eric asked, trying hard to sound casual. "Or wolves?"

She shook her head.

"So if they heard us land here," I said, getting back to our task, "then their village, or camp, or whatever, can't be too far away. That may work to our advantage, as long as we don't get caught first."

"Yeah," Eric said, smearing insect repellent on his own legs, "but we're from the twenty-first century and we've watched thousands of hours of TV. We can outsmart them."

I wasn't entirely sure about Eric's logic, but he did have a point. The local Natives were familiar with the area, but so were we. They would be trying to catch us, but we were on to them. Sure, they were adults and professional hunters, and we were just kids—but we were kids from the future.

"I think they will be behind us soon," Anna said. "We should move away from here."

Since she had spent two days successfully avoiding capture, we trusted her instincts and lifted our packs.

"Let's do what they do in the movies," Eric suggested. "We'll stomp down into the river, like we're crossing it and continuing north. But as soon as we're in the water, we'll turn right and head south. They can't track us in water."

Anna nodded.

"That may not fool them forever," I said, "but it should buy us enough time to figure something out."

Twenty minutes later we were still on the same side of the Kilmeny River and about half a mile south. We slogged our way into the pine trees above the bank and rested. We all drank from our water bottles and shared cookies from the box we'd taken from Eric's kitchen. Anna lost the look of fear and nervousness that had been on her face back at the stones. She told us about her father's obsession with the pillars, and how every time he had the chance, they would fly to one of the sites to examine and re-examine the curious stones.

"And that's why you were in Sultana?" I asked. "At the cemetery?"

"Yes." Anna took a sip from her water bottle and nodded.

Eric found a comfortable-looking place on the ground and sat down. "That is so cool," he said. "Flying around the world and having all sorts of adventures."

I craned my neck and snuck a peek down the river to make sure we weren't being tailed. "Yeah,"

I agreed. "Sure we travelled here to the past, but that doesn't even really count, because we're still in Sultana."

Anna smiled, as if sympathizing.

"What about school?" Eric asked. "Don't you have to go to school in Germany?"

"Not anymore. My mother used to be a teacher and now I am home-schooled."

"Are you kidding me?" Eric said. "You mean you never have to go to any boring classes?"

"I do not go to classes," Anna said, "but I still do all my lessons and assignments and tests."

"Come on," Eric teased, "really?" He wedged a cookie into his mouth and chewed.

"Yes, really. The only difference is that my home is my classroom."

"That's still pretty cool," I said, though I didn't think I'd be able to concentrate on my boring geometry homework, sitting in my bedroom, looking out the window.

Eric peeked around some willow shrubs to get a better view of the river downstream. Suddenly he froze. "There! There they are!" He pointed to where we had pretended to cross the river.

I dug out Eric's binoculars and crawled over to him. I zoomed in on the search party. "Five guys," I said, "no, make that six. And, Anna, I think you're right. Native North Americans." Anna joined us and I passed her the field glasses.

Anna sighed, looking at her pursuers. "Yes, that is them. They are the ones who took Rachel away."

"Where could they have taken her?" I said to Eric. "If you had to set up a camp in Sultana—in our Sultana—where would you put it?"

"Maybe by Bruce and Marg's house . . ." Eric stopped and shook his head. "I mean, where the Kilmeny River joins the Red River. The fishing there is good, and the bugs aren't too bad because of the constant breeze."

"Yeah," I agreed. "There really isn't a better place than that. And it would be close enough for them to hear whatever they heard when we arrived." I took a final glance downriver and watched with satisfaction as the group moved north, trying to pick up our tracks.

"Where is this place?" Anna asked. "Where the rivers connect?"

Eric strapped on his backpack and pointed

northwest. Anna and I looked at the blue sky through a break in the forest above us. When I squinted, I saw fingers of light grey smoke drifting into the air, a mile from where we were standing.

Eric grinned. "That's a sure sign of a camp. We need to get there and take a look around."

I nodded. "But I don't think we should all go."

"You mean we should split up?" Anna looked stricken.

"Yeah," I said. "If the three of us go anywhere together, our movements will scream our presence to these guys. Remember, they're expert trackers and hunters. They'll see us, they'll hear us, and heck, they'll probably even smell us before we get within a hundred feet of their camp."

We sat quietly in the afternoon sun, contemplating our next move.

"I think I should go alone and check out their camp," I said. "See if Rachel's there."

Eric opened his mouth to protest, but I cut him off. "My skin is way darker than yours. You almost glow in the night."

Anna looked at Eric's blond hair and pale skin, and then laughed. "It is true," she said. "And it is almost a full moon too. They might think you are an evil spirit and kill you if they see you tonight."

Eric didn't like the idea of being left out. "But if I come," he said, "I could create a massive diversion while you rescue Rachel and—"

"We're not rescuing her, not until we know what's going on," I reminded him. "And if two of us go, it only doubles the risk of us getting caught."

"He is right," Anna said. "Two people will make twice as much noise in the night. And the night here is very quiet—no wind, no birds, no other sounds. I could go, but you know this area, and it is dark. I would likely become lost."

So that settled it—I would wait until dark, and I would have to be more careful than I'd ever been in my life.

CHAPTER 5

"MORE MUD, ANNA," Eric said. "And more moss and junk."

It was almost midnight, and Anna and Eric were prepping me for my mission. Ten minutes earlier, my dark brown T-shirt and khaki-coloured shorts looked brand new—now they looked like I'd found them in a dumpster. We even pounded both pieces of clothing with dirt and leaves, to get rid of any "foreign" smells.

Now we were working on the finishing touches that would make my dark skin even darker. Anna smeared my legs with dirt, while Eric dripped sticky pine tree sap on my shirt. On each tarry blob, Eric pressed something from the forest floor—moss, leaves, bark, and so on.

Making me look invisible seemed to take

everyone's mind off our problems—for the moment, anyway.

"You look terrific," Eric beamed. "Even if they stare right at you, they won't see you."

We'd found a tree that had been struck by lightning, and both Eric and Anna used the charred wood to plaster my face with black soot. "I'm just glad it's warm out tonight," I said.

"Yes," Anna agreed, painting my ears black, "last night felt much cooler."

"They probably won't be expecting us to backtrack and sneak up on them," Eric said. "But you'd still better be super-careful and—"

"I know, I know," I snapped, and then grimaced when I heard my harsh voice. The idea of us being stuck here forever was getting to me. I took a deep breath and added, "But if I'm not back by morning, you and Anna better make plans to leave without me. There's no point in all four of us being stranded here."

Anna and Eric looked at each other. "We'll see," Eric said. He gave me his pocket knife (his birthday present, by the way), and I shoved it deep in my pocket. I felt a lot better knowing I was armed and dangerous. Okay, maybe I wasn't dangerous, but at least I was armed. I took off my wristwatch and jammed it into my pants too. I didn't want the luminous dial attracting attention. Like I said, I was going to be careful.

"Does that clock have an alarm?" Anna asked, pointing at my pants.

"Clock?" I said. "Huh?"

"Will it beep every hour?"

I laughed. "Oh, I see. No, my watch doesn't do anything fancy, it's just waterproof."

The only other thing I took with me was the walkie-talkie. I slid it into my zippered pocket—thank goodness for cargo pants—and said, "Remember, the radio is for emergency use by me only. Don't call me no matter what, or you'll give away my position for sure."

"Understood," Anna said. "I will keep my radio on, but I will not try to call you."

I drank half a bottle of water and made my way down to the river. The moon was below the trees, but I was still able to make good time in the darkness. When I got close to the spot where the highway bridge in Sultana would eventually be, I climbed the bank and entered the forest.

I stuck to the open areas, slowly and quietly winding my way toward the fork in the river. With each step, I pressed down lightly to minimize the crunch of leaves and twigs. And when I thought my footfall was too loud, I paused and waited nervously for warning shouts. After thirty minutes, I began to catch the faint smell of wood smoke. I stopped again. Was it good or bad that I could smell their fire? The little hairs on the back of my neck tingled and sprang to attention.

I closed my eyes and tried to concentrate. Think, Cody, think. What was it we learned in Boy Scouts?

That's right, I thought, as I remembered. If you're trying to sneak up on an animal, you want to have the wind in your face, so that the animal can't smell you. I allowed myself a quick grin. There was no wind—only a slight breeze—but the smoke I could smell meant I was downwind and moving in the right direction. Perfect.

The nearly full moon rose higher as I prowled ever closer. With each pace, I gave myself more time to wait, listen, and plan my next step. Suddenly, a wave of laughter reached my ears. The camp was close.

I took a cautious step and listened. Crickets and

other insects buzzed softly around me, and I was sure the bats were out now too. Their eerie, black bodies flew in sloppy circles around the canopy as they munched on mosquitoes and other night insects.

I took another ten slow steps and listened some more. I could recognize different voices now, though the bugs were still competing for my attention.

WAIT! What was that?!

I was so busy trying to angle my ears closer, I almost lost track of my other senses. That was when I caught a slight movement near a tree, thirty steps ahead. I froze, sank to a crouch and waited. Staring at the spot, I urged my eyes to focus. But there was nothing visible in the shadowy night. Had I imagined it? I willed my ears to listen even harder, but heard no noise. Still, I didn't dare move. I had seen enough movies where someone gave away their position by being impatient and moving too soon. I wasn't about to make that blunder. We had way too much at stake!

If someone was there, they'd be patient too. So I waited, listened and watched.

Fifteen minutes went by. My legs had cramped,

and it felt like nearly enough time had passed. But nearly wasn't good enough, so I stayed frozen. I trusted my eyes and my instincts—because I had seen something.

The tree I was staring at suddenly came to life. Only it wasn't a tree! It was a man cloaked in fur, and he had been squatting near the ground. He stood up and grunted something in a language I didn't understand to a second person only three feet away. I watched as they both moved like ghosts toward their camp.

That was way too close. I had almost walked smack into two lookouts. Thank goodness for my camouflage.

That was my first close call. The second one happened twenty minutes later.

After the sentries left, I prowled around the perimeter of the camp on my knees. I watched the camp carefully for signs of Rachel—and then another man walked out of a tent and headed straight toward me.

For a moment, I wavered between fleeing and holding my ground. If I ran, he would see me for sure, and then I would have the whole tribe after me. But if I held my ground, he might walk straight into me.

I had to take that chance and trust my disguise would hide me. But that didn't slow my heartbeat one bit.

When he was five feet away, he stopped and began to pee. I closed my eyes so he couldn't see their whites glowing in the moonlight. I cringed at the sound of liquid hitting the soil. Holding my breath, I avoided the impulse to cry "P-U!" When I finally heard him turn and walk away, I opened my eyes again. This was nuts!

The camp was smaller than I'd imagined. There were seven teepee tents set up to form roughly the shape of a semi-circle. Even in the moonlight, I could see that each tent was elaborately decorated with paintings. Beyond the tents I saw the final proof I was looking for. The Red and Kilmeny Rivers were right where they were supposed to be—just like in our Sultana. The riverbank in the distance was lined with several birch bark canoes. A cooking fire burned near the middle of the camp.

I couldn't see Rachel among the adults and children. Wait! The second tent from the river had a guard posted near the front opening. Maybe Rachel was in there?

I crawled into a thicket of brush and settled in to observe the camp.

I couldn't see anything sinister or war-like about the group. Women chatted quietly around the fire—some were rocking infants. A few older kids were gathered around a Native Elder, like they were listening to a story. Others headed off to bed, and I'm sure some were in the teepees already asleep. The whole scene looked pretty peaceful.

But they had Rachel, and we wanted her back.

The tent flap opened on the second teepee. I held my breath. Rachel emerged from the shelter, followed by a Native who was probably a foot taller than me. He was dressed more or less like the other men, except he had a red cap on his head. It looked like something Ebenezer Scrooge might wear to bed. The red cap got me thinking about something I had learned in school, but the memory I was groping for slipped away.

Anyway, the tall guy said something to an old lady who had been poking the fire. She stopped what she was doing and led Rachel into the forest. Rachel obediently followed, and they both returned five minutes later.

Rachel wasn't tied up. In fact, except for being watched by the tall guy—and probably by everyone else in the camp—she looked at ease. I was relieved to see that she looked healthy and alert. She walked to the fire and hovered around it. Some of the other women came to talk to her and offered her food or water, but Rachel declined with a shake of her head. She often looked up at the sky or around the camp.

Anna told us that Rachel had been unconscious when they carried her away, which I guess explained why Rachel didn't just run into the forest as fast as she could—she had no idea where she was or where she had landed. And since she didn't even know we were here with her, it made a lot of sense for her to stay with the Natives.

I desperately wanted to scream, "We're here, Rachel! Don't worry, we'll rescue you!" But of course, I kept my mouth shut. Poor Rachel.

How the heck could we get her away from them? Would they just let her leave? Could we trade something for her? But what could we offer them?

I looked around the camp for anything that might

help us rescue Rachel. Thanks to the stars, the moon, and the flames from the fire, I had a great view of the people near the campfire. But there was something about that tall Native—the one who had followed Rachel out of the tent—that grabbed my attention. He just looked different from the others around him.

I squinted through the night at the stranger. I wished I'd brought the binoculars with me so I could really zoom in on his features. He was close enough that I could see he had long dark hair poking out from under his toque. And he also had a longer nose, paler skin, and a bigger head than anyone else in camp. Then, when he turned so that the fire illuminated the front of his body, I saw all I needed to see—a colourful sash wrapped around his waist.

He was a voyageur!

He was not a North American Native!

I thought back to history class and tried to concentrate. If the man with the red cap really was a voyageur, and not with the Woodland Cree—the tribe I suspected these Natives belonged to—we must have gone back to the 1700s or 1800s.

On the other hand, he could also be a fellow time traveller. Right? In which case, we may have travelled back hundreds of years before that. As I lay in hiding, I began thinking about what Bruno had tried to tell us just before we disappeared at the stones. I had been so distracted, his warning barely registered in my brain. But now—now I was sure he was urging us to be wary of other people from the future.

It doesn't matter, I decided, shaking my head. I knew this man spoke either French or English, and that little piece of information was enough for me to form a rescue plan. I fine-tuned the scheme in my head while I waited for the camp to shut down for the night. One hour later, as the two lookouts made a final sweep of the perimeter and turned in for the night, I felt confident we could get Rachel and return home.

I gave them another fifteen minutes to zonk out and then I slid into their camp. Tiptoeing between two tents, I went straight to a dead poplar tree near the centre of their encampment. It had a million holes in it from woodpeckers or squirrels trying to use its remains.

I dug my walkie-talkie out from my pocket and carefully turned it on. I was terrified it would let out an electronic squawk, but it didn't. So far so good. Reaching as high as I could, I placed it in a knot hole and covered the opening with a thin layer of moss.

I left the camp as cautiously as I had entered it. When I was sure I was out of earshot of anyone in the tents, I picked up the pace and jogged to the Kilmeny. I hid in the bush there for twenty minutes to be certain I wasn't being followed. I didn't want to be the dummy who got us all captured.

After I caught my breath again, I ran down to the river and then south along the bank to Anna and Eric.

"Pssst!" I whispered, when I got near the spot where I had left them. "Eric? Anna?"

"What took you so long?" Eric said, stepping from behind a spruce tree. "I was starting to think you got lost." He led me another hundred feet into the forest, where he and Anna had made a small fire. Anna was asleep under a thin, silver thermal blanket. She was using a backpack as a pillow.

After two sleepless nights in the bush, Anna deserved some rest. We could brief her in the morning. "They have her," I said quietly to Eric.

He sighed and placed another stick in the fire. "Tell me everything."

He listened intently while I recounted my close calls with the Natives. He laughed when I explained that my disguise was so good I almost got peed on. And his eyes grew huge when I told him that another time traveller might be living among the Natives. I finished by saying, "I think they're Woodland Cree."

Eric nodded. "Teepees?"

"Yeah." We had learned in school that the Ojibwe lived in domed lodges called wigwams, while the Cree preferred to live in teepees.

"So," he said, "do you have any ideas for getting Rachel back?"

I grinned. "Yeah, actually I do. But it's such a long shot we should have a Plan B too—just in case."

I told Eric how I had stashed the walkie-talkie in the tree, and what I wanted to do tomorrow.

"If that's Plan A," he said, shaking his head, "we'll definitely need a backup plan."

We made ourselves comfortable around the fire and tried to get some sleep. But as exhausted as we were, I don't think either one of us slept very much. We had way too much at stake. The rest of our lives would be determined by what happened in the morning. If we didn't rescue Rachel, and if we didn't all make it back to the stones soon, we'd be stuck here for a long time, maybe forever.

I woke up sweating. The sun had managed to find a gap in the trees, and it was blasting my face with heat. I sat up, rubbed my eyes and wiped my grimy forehead.

"Good morning," Anna said. She must have just returned from the river. Her face was clean and some of her brown hair was still wet.

I shook Eric awake, and we trundled down to the river to wash ourselves. Only it took me a lot longer to scrub away all the soot and junk I had smeared on my skin the night before. But all the rubbing and cleaning sure woke me up.

When I returned to the bush, I filled Anna in on everything I had seen last night.

"I am glad Rachel is safe and close by," she said with visible relief. She still felt responsible for not being able to save Rachel. "But how are we going to rescue her?"

We briefly told Anna what we knew about voyageurs, and I explained how I identified the tall man from his clothes—the red cap, the sash, the pants, and so forth.

"So . . . we have a contact in the camp?" Anna said. "This fur trader person?"

I shrugged. "We might."

"If we can trust him," Eric added.

"I believe I saw that same man at the pillars," Anna said. "He did not have the red hat on when he took Rachel, but I am sure it was the same person."

"Was he . . . " Eric searched for the right words, "was he mean to her?"

"No," Anna said. "He treated her kindly and with great care."

"He'd better have," Eric said.

Anna turned to me. "Now, tell me about your plan."

"Last night I hid one of our walkie-talkies in a tree, inside their camp, and today I want to walk into their camp and ask for Rachel's return. If they refuse, Eric is going to use his walkie-talkie to trick them into thinking the tree is talking to them."

"A talking tree?" Anna said. "Why a tree?"

"It doesn't matter what is talking," I explained. "We

learned in school that the Cree have a strong bond with nature. They believe that everything in the natural world has a spirit, and that all spirits have to be respected. If we can convince them that the spirit of the trees is asking for Rachel's release, then—"

Anna held up her hand to stop me. "But you do not know how to speak the Cree language."

"That's where you come in," Eric said.

"Your dad told us you're great with languages," I said. "Is your French as good as your English?"

Anna grinned. "My French is even better. My mother was born in Switzerland—in a French-speaking town—and we often speak French with each other."

"Good," I said. "Because we'll need you to communicate with Red Hat in French, and then he can translate into Cree."

Eric chuckled. "'Red Hat,' eh? I like that."

Anna ignored Eric. "He looks like he is in his twenties, so if he is a time traveller, he may have been here for years. I wonder if he still speaks French?"

"I sure hope so," Eric said, chewing on a granola bar. "That's a critical part of the plan."

Eric and I slung our bags on our backs, and we all

headed north toward Rachel and the Natives. "And remember," I said to Eric, "when we get close, stay way back. It's probably best if you approach from the west and then hide. There are a couple of good spots in that area, where you should be able to see everything and still hear me when I yell."

"No problem," he said.

"And don't say anything until I tell you to."

Eric nodded and began walking north.

When we were five minutes from the camp, Eric left Anna and me and headed west to approach the camp from the far side. We gave him fifteen minutes to get in position. Then Anna and I did the unthinkable: we walked straight into the camp, in the daylight, with no disguise, to save Rachel.

CHAPTER 6

THE NATIVES WERE so unprepared for our arrival, they didn't know how to react. A few people working around the fire simply froze and stared at us.

I put my bag down at the base of the old poplar tree and yelled, "HELLO!"

A second later, Anna yelled, "BONJOUR! HELLO!"

We had everyone's attention now. People came running from all directions. Tent flaps opened, and Natives poured out and surrounded us. Some of the men grabbed spears and formed a sloppy circle around Anna and me. Kids who had been playing in the water came running to see the pale-skinned strangers, but hid behind their mothers and grandmothers and great-grandmothers.

"Cody!" Rachel bullied her way through the crowd and ran up to me, her face full of relief. "I knew you would come for me! I knew it!" She gave me such a tight hug, I thought I felt my ribs creak.

I whispered, "Eric's with me too, but don't look around for him—he's hiding in the forest."

Rachel released me and stared for a second at Anna with a confused look. But then her eyes brightened. She gave Anna a quick hug too and said, "I'm glad you're safe."

A grumpy-looking guy—probably the chief—pulled Rachel back and barked something at us in Cree.

Anna ignored him and yelled again. "BONJOUR!"

Red Hat pushed his way forward and glared down at us.

Anna asked him something in French, but the expression on his grumpy face didn't change.

"I don't think he's French," Anna said to me.

Oh no!

The chief started getting twitchy and yelled at us for a second time in Cree. I don't think he liked not knowing what was going on. A thin smile spread across Red Hat's face. It looked a little sinister, but then again, some people smiled that way.

The plan was falling apart, and I knew I had to do

something fast. "We have come for the girl!" I yelled, pointing at Rachel. Even if they couldn't understand English, I reasoned, they might still understand the message, if you know what I mean.

I think the chief got the gist of that, because he nodded. But then he said something to his people and laughed. In fact, he laughed so hard it became contagious, and soon everyone was creased up and laughing at us. The only people who weren't laughing were Anna, Rachel, Red Hat, and me.

The situation was going from bad to worse.

When the laughter subsided, I spun around and pointed at the old tree. As loud as I could, I yelled, "Okay, Eric, start saying something. And you better make it good!"

The walkie-talkie I'd hidden in the tree the night before came to life. "Hi, Rachel," the tree said. "Don't worry about anything. I know this looks like a goofy plan, but it should work."

A collective murmur rose around us. Rachel looked at me dubiously and then at the tree. Clearly, she had little faith in our escape scheme.

When the tree—I mean, Eric—stopped talking, I yelled, "The tree spirit wants Rachel to leave with us."

The chief gave a lengthy lecture to his people, turned to face us again and shook his giant head.

Some of the kids grew bored with all the talking and drifted back to the water for a swim.

I turned to the tree and yelled. "They don't believe us, Eric! Say something else and try to sound like you're mad!"

The tree spoke again, angrily. "Listen up, you bozos! I want my sister back now. I like her—sometimes I even love her, but not very often—and I want her back!"

Rachel let out a soft moan and covered her eyes. One of the older women standing next to her rubbed her back to comfort her.

The chief glared at the tree until an old man whispered something in his ear. The chief nodded, cupped his hands together and blew into the space between his thumbs. The eerie call of a loon sounded from his hands. He then yelled across the river in Cree.

WHOOO-OOO-HOOOOOO. The distinct cry of a loon echoed across the water.

That's great. That's just great, I thought.

The chief, of course, looked pretty smug. He said

something to his people, and murmurs of agreement rose around him.

I suspect he said something like, "This kid can talk to the tree spirits, but I can talk to the animal spirits."

That was when the tree decided to speak again. "Okay, Cody, from where I'm hiding, it doesn't look like this is working. Let's go to Plan B."

The warrior-types in the band had already realized we weren't a threat and put down their spears and bows. Sure, we were strange—and probably a huge nuisance—but it was obvious we couldn't hurt them.

I pulled Rachel's digital camera from my pocket and turned it on. The tribesmen who were still hanging around leaned in to look when the lens opened up and expanded outward. I scrolled back through the pictures and found a selfie she had taken. I zoomed in so that her head filled the small LCD display.

"LOOK!" I screamed, holding up the camera so that everyone could see Rachel on the monitor. "Her spirit remains in another world. She is not complete with your people. We must take her back!"

The chief rubbed his chin thoughtfully and then picked his teeth with one of the many claws strung around his neck. I held my breath while he considered this latest development.

After several excruciating minutes, the chief stuck out his hand. I passed him the camera and let him look at Rachel's "trapped" spirit. He felt the weight of the camera and turned it over and over in his leathery palm.

Without warning, he placed it on a rock and smashed it with another stone. CRUNCH!

"HEY!" I screamed. "That was her birthday present!" I know that was an irrelevant comment, but it made me mad to see him destroy Rachel's camera.

"Well," said the tree, "I guess Rachel's spirit is now free." But the talking tree didn't impress anyone anymore, and no one even looked at it. In fact, everyone except Red Hat left to continue with whatever camp chores they were working on. And, speaking of Red Hat, it was almost like he was assigned to shadow Rachel, always staying within arm's reach, ready to grab her if she tried to make a run for it. It was kind of annoying, to tell you the truth.

Eric jogged into the camp a minute later and joined the four of us. Red Hat seemed slightly alarmed by the arrival of yet another kid, but he didn't run off to fetch the chief. I noticed a few people in the camp look up and point, but they weren't intrigued enough to walk back to check Eric out. I guess the novelty of strange children showing up had already worn off.

After giving his sister a quick hug, Eric said, "I thought of something while I was watching you guys."

"What's that?" I said, sneaking suspicious glances at the voyageur, or time traveller, or whatever he was.

"I still think this guy," Eric pointed at Red Hat with his thumb, "is a voyageur. And I think he speaks English or French, or both. He must."

"But he has not said a word," Anna said.

Rachel squinted at her brother. "Are you saying he's pretending he doesn't understand us?"

We all looked over at the tall man, standing three feet behind Rachel. He continued to stare at us blankly, not saying a word.

"No," Eric whispered. "I think he doesn't understand our English or Anna's French, because it's different."

Anna slowly began to nod. "You could be right."

"You lost me," I said. "What's different?"

"The language," Eric said. "Think of how different

English must have sounded three hundred years ago. If we time-travelled to London back then, no one would understand what the heck we were saying either."

I scratched my head. "You really think English and French have evolved that much?"

"There's only one way to find out," Eric said. He turned and looked up at Red Hat.

Rachel shrugged.

Eric cleared his throat and yelled, "'Ello, gov'na, cannest thou understand me?"

"What the heck are you doing?" Rachel said.

Eric held up his hand for Rachel to be patient. "Kind sir," Eric babbled on, "what be your name, pray tell?"

Anna giggled.

"Oh, brother," I said.

But Eric continued, determined to communicate with the voyageur. "'Tis most splendid if you would speakest. What say you, My Lord?"

"Forget it, Eric," Rachel said. "That's ridiculous."

"You're right," he admitted. "I don't think he understands English. Anna will have to talk like that in French now. "

"ENOUGH!" Red Hat bellowed suddenly. "I can not take zis . . . zis nonsense any more." He spoke broken English with a thick French accent, but we could definitely understand him. And he could obviously understand us without us having to talk like Robin Hood or King Arthur.

"You speak English?" Rachel said, shocked.

He ignored that and said, "You will all stay 'ere. And no one is to go to zee stones."

He walked up to the tree, stared at it for a minute and then reached into the hole and pulled out my walkie-talkie. After studying the gadget for a while, he passed it back to me. "Stupeed parlour tricks," he added.

"Actually, it's a walkie-talkie," Eric mumbled.

"Why are you all 'ere?" he demanded.

"You speak English?" Rachel said again. "Why didn't you say something to me earlier?"

"I . . . I am sorry," he stammered. "I was not sure of your purpose."

"Purpose?" Rachel said in disbelief. "There is no purpose. We just want to go back—back to our time. Anna and I accidentally fell into the wormhole, and Cody and Eric came to bring us back."

I helpfully pointed at the three of us as Rachel said each of our names.

"Worm . . . hole?" he said slowly. "Is zat what brought me to zis time?"

Anna nodded. "Yes, and you can come back with us if you want."

I was about to point out that he couldn't, on account of his age, but then he said, "I 'ave no desire to return. My life before was nozing but toil. I am 'appy 'ere. The Cree respect me, and I respect zem."

"What is your name?" Anna asked.

"I was called Léon Leblanc. But now I am known as Gift-From-Zee-Stones."

"Okay, Léon," Eric said, seeming to get more impatient with each minute. "If you want to stay here, we won't stop you. But we need to get out of here. So if you could convince the chief to let us go, you'd be doing us a huge favour."

Léon (a.k.a. Gift-From-The-Stones, a.k.a. Red Hat) didn't say anything, so we just stood there waiting and worrying. The only noise that reached us was the kids swimming and laughing in the river, around the bend.

"We only want to go home," Anna reminded him.

"But if the chief won't let us go, we'll miss our chance to go back. Will you help us?"

Eric shifted from foot to foot, like he had to pee. "I'll back in a sec," he said. "I gotta pee." (Told you.) He jogged around the bend and disappeared.

Léon looked down his nose at each of us. "I will go and speak with zee chief. Stay near zee camp or . . . or zee chief will not be 'appy." He turned around and left us to go search for the chief, who must have returned to his tent, because I couldn't see him anywhere.

When he was gone, Rachel said, "I don't trust that guy."

"Yeah," I admitted "but at least he's offered to help us now."

Rachel didn't look convinced. "He spent a long time pretending he couldn't speak English or French—enough time to learn everything he could. And we have no idea what he really told the chief when he was talking to him."

I considered that as I watched Léon disappear inside a teepee. "We just have to be careful. For now, we better pretend we trust him, and hope he can help us." I looked over the camp, which had returned to its usual rhythm. "We can't make a run to the stones right now anyway, not with everyone watching."

Rachel nodded. "We need to be patient, but we also need to be ready."

CHAPTER 7

I LEFT ANNA and Rachel by the dead tree, and headed off to find Eric. He'd been gone a long time, and we were starting to think he was lost. I could have used the walkie-talkie to call him, but after seeing what the chief had done to Rachel's camera, I didn't want to risk losing that too. Plus, we should save the batteries.

I left the camp and walked west, where I'd seen Eric disappear. I expected to see him around every bend in the trail—only I didn't. So I headed away from the camp, moving closer and closer to the Red River. I climbed a small rise and turned around to get my bearings. I could see the whole camp, and even without the binoculars, I could see Rachel and Anna standing by the tree.

Come on, Eric, where are you?

I had started to take my walkie-talkie from my pants pocket when I heard a muffled noise coming from down by the river.

Eric?

I fought my way through the scratchy shrubs to get down to the bank.

"Thank God!" Eric cried. "What took you so long?"

It took me a few seconds to understand what I was seeing. Eric was on his knees next to an unconscious girl and was desperately trying to revive her. A boy and another girl stood by nervously, whimpering and mumbling in Cree. All three kids looked like they were about six or seven years old.

"They were swimming," Eric said, performing quick compressions on her little chest with one hand. "Something must have happened . . . They started screaming . . ." He gave me a desperate look. "I had to help her. She's not breathing . . . and . . . I can't feel a pulse!"

"No pulse?" I mumbled.

Eric nodded and switched hands. "But check yourself," he said. "Maybe I just couldn't find it."

I dropped to my knees across from Eric, on the other side of the girl. I checked all the heartbeat pulse points we had learned about in our school CPR class—neck, wrist, and ankle—but I couldn't feel the thump of blood pushing through her body. Nothing.

Eric was soaked with sweat. "Here," I said, "let me take over. Take a break." I gently pinched her tiny nose like we were taught in Health class and blew twice into her mouth. Her lips were cold too, and I wondered how long she had been underwater.

Oh no! Was she already dead?

I shook my head and took a deep breath. We couldn't panic now—her life depended on us staying calm. I pushed down on her small chest with another thirty quick compressions. Push hard, push fast. Push hard, push fast. Our instructor's chant kept going through my head. I also remembered his warning that it wasn't uncommon to crack ribs while performing CPR. That didn't make me feel any better. Push hard, push fast.

I paused to see if her chest was rising on its own. No response.

"I tried calling you on the walkie-talkie," Eric said, huffing and puffing to catch his breath, "but . . . "

"Yeah," I mumbled, "it was turned off." I repeated

the resuscitation steps over and over and over—until I was exhausted too—but she still wasn't breathing.

Eric nudged me aside and took over again.

The girl was turning blue, and I was getting frantic. I had never seen anyone die before, and I realized now how awful it would be to watch her life drift away, especially because she was young and helpless. We had to save her.

As soon as Eric finished his compressions, I leaned over and blew into her mouth. Looking at her chest, I waited. And then—was I seeing things?—it rose and fell again, by itself.

She was alive!

Eric rolled her over onto her side. "Oh man. It worked. She's actually breathing." Our patient coughed and gagged, trying to clear her water-logged lungs.

The two kids waiting next to us stared in wonder. Then, they jumped up and down, hugging each other and laughing.

We watched, fascinated, as the girl who had been so close to death regained her colour and warmed up quickly under the sun. She continued coughing for a while, but she seemed to be out of danger now.

We all sat and waited for her to recover fully. And after twenty minutes, she sat up and began speaking to her companions.

"Hopefully," Eric said, "they'll run back and tell their parents about this awesome miracle we performed. Then they'll let us leave for sure."

I shook my head and studied the kids. "In the movies that sometimes backfires."

"It can't," Eric said. "We saved her life with some twenty-first-century CPR. It was a textbook rescue."

"It sure was," I agreed. "But they may see it differently. What if they think she almost died because we brought bad luck to the band? Or what if they think we were trying to suck the life out of her and failed?"

"Hmmm," Eric grumbled.

"I say we try to keep this quiet. We've got enough to worry about without having to try to explain how CPR works."

"Okay," Eric said. "It's just a shame that we won't be showered with gifts and rewards for our good deed."

With that settled, I turned to the three children, put my finger up to my lips and went "Shhh." I wasn't sure if that was a timeless indicator to keep quiet, but it was worth a try.

The kids looked at each other and then back at us. One of them shrugged.

Eric tried next. He pointed to the camp and then used his hand to mimic a talking gesture—a mouth opening and closing. He shook his head with a stern look on his face, emphasizing that this would be a bad thing to do.

The boy pointed toward the camp, nodded and then repeated my "Shhh" gesture. I suppose even kids in the past know how to keep secrets from parents and adults. Our victim coughed up some more water, smiled and held her finger to her lips. I think the only thing that kept her from saying "Shhh" was her tired throat.

Anyway, we were all on the same page now.

Eric and I followed the children back to camp. The girl we revived stopped every twenty feet for a good fit of coughing, but she seemed to be in good spirits. Eric had tried to carry her—thinking she might be too weak to stand—but she squirmed away, eager to walk with her friends. I guess she had had enough attention for one morning. The slow trip back allowed plenty of time for me to fill Eric in on what had happened at the tree.

"And now," I concluded, "he's talking to the chief to see if we can leave."

"I guess that's progress," Eric said.

"But we can't trust him," I whispered. "He might be hiding something else. So we have to be careful when he's near."

"That makes sense," Eric said.

Rachel ran over to us as soon as we entered the camp. "Gosh," she said, "what took you two so long? We were getting worried."

"It's a long story," Eric said, grinning, "and I'll tell you about it later. But we're both heroes."

Rachel looked at her brother with confusion. "What are you talking—?"

"Children!" Léon waved us over to one of the tents. "Come 'ere."

"This better be good news," I said, heading toward the teepee. "We're running out of time."

Léon glared at Eric and then scowled at me, but he didn't question our lengthy absence from the camp. He held back the tent flap, and we all piled into the chief's home. The chief, a few women, and a bunch of other senior Natives were already sitting around in a circle. They had left a gap in the circle, and Léon ordered us to sit there. The tent was smoky, hot, and packed with people.

When everyone had settled in, the chief started things off with a long speech. My hands were sweating fiercely, and I tried hard to keep them from shaking as I listened. We had no idea what Léon may have told the chief. I was worried we had made a mistake trusting him—instead of making a run for it—and I sensed that time was slipping by. We needed to be on our way, and we didn't have time for any more shenanigans or complications from the chief.

Finally he stopped talking, and Léon summarized his lecture for us in English. "Zee chief 'az reconsidered. He does not understand why zee spirits would want such pale, sick-looking children back. You are all welcome to stay 'ere forever, but zee chief will leave zee final decision to zee spirit of zee stones."

"What does that mean?" I asked.

"It means," Léon said, "if you can all pass through zee pillars, zat is a sign zat zee spirits must want you back. And zat is fine with zee chief. But if you fail to travel back to your world, zee chief will take zat as a message from zee spirits zat zey don't want you and you must remain 'ere."

I couldn't believe it. That was exactly what we wanted! "That sounds reasonable," I said, struggling to keep my voice even.

"And if you leave," Léon continued, "'e wants you to tell zee spirits to stop sending 'im troublesome gifts."

I exchanged glances with Eric. There was no way we could guarantee that, but we could tell Bruno when we returned. "Sure," Eric said, "whatever."

I felt that I should show my appreciation, so I said, "Tell the chief we thank him, and we will ask all the spirits to bless him and his people with excellent hunting, fishing, and health."

I stood up, hoping that would signal an end to the meeting. But it didn't.

The chief pointed at the ground, the universal sign for "sit your butt back down." So I sat my butt back down. He solemnly spoke to me, and then I waited to find out what he'd solemnly said from Léon.

"Zee chief said zat you should show your gratitude immediately by presenting 'im with a gift."

Eric groaned and said, "What a guy."

Rachel jabbed Eric in ribs. "Don't make him mad."

"He can't understand me," Eric mumbled.

"I know," Rachel said, "but a groan is rude in any language."

"I suppose," I said to Eric, "I can give him your pocket knife."

Eric groaned again, only louder.

Rachel nodded.

I reached into my pocket and pulled out Eric's birthday present, the folding pocket knife. We hadn't used it for anything yet, so the metal still sparkled like new. As soon as I flipped out a blade, the Natives "Ahhh'd," appreciating the knife's shininess. I folded and unfolded it several times, so everyone could admire the craftsmanship. Then I flicked open the steel a final time, picked up a piece of firewood and shaved off a foot-long curl of wood.

The chief laughed and clapped his hands together like it was his birthday present. He snatched the knife from my hand as I was tucking the blade away, and it accidentally cut his thumb. He grinned and proudly showed the group the blood flowing down his hand.

I guess he liked it.

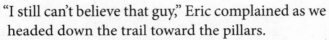

"I still can't believe that guy," Eric complained as we headed down the trail toward the pillars.

"Just let it go already," Rachel said.

But he wouldn't. "He kidnaps you, he smashes your camera, and then he has the nerve to demand a gift—my gift."

"You've got at least three more jackknives at home," Rachel said.

"But I really liked that one," he whined.

"As long as we don't miss the wormhole," I said, looking up at the sky, "I don't care what he takes from us."

"They should have had a massive feast for us—like in the movies. Why couldn't they make a huge fire and barbeque steaks, and hamburgers, and chicken wings, and—?"

"I do not think they have any of those foods," Anna interrupted.

"Well, they could have tried," Eric whined. "Everyone knows how to make a burger."

Anna laughed and said, "Maybe you are right, Eric. The bun could be made from the bannock, and if they mashed up deer meat, they could form meat patties."

Eric laughed too. "It's not a Big Mac, but I don't feel super-picky right now."

I was pretty sure we would make it to the stones before the meteor shower ended, but we all hustled down the trail at a near-run anyway. Léon was the only one from the Cree camp accompanying the four of us. The chief wasn't into emotional farewells—thank goodness. He simply waved us away with a flick of his fingers.

Léon led the way through the forest. I felt a bit bad for not trusting him, but we weren't out of the woods yet—literally. Anything could still happen. We let Léon get far enough ahead so that he couldn't hear what we were saying. Then we did our best to fill Rachel in on everything that had happened since she disappeared at the cemetery.

When I finished, Rachel said, "So during the Perseid meteor shower, that wormhole opens up in the centre of the stones?"

"Yes, exactly," I said, stepping over a fallen oak tree. "And that wormhole is a shortcut to the past."

Eric added, "But that only happens once a year."

"Actually," Anna said, "the portal may open many times during the year. But I think Papa was only able to translate a few of the symbols. Other cultures may have observed the wormhole opening at other times of the year too."

Rachel nodded. "So the ancient people who painted and carved those symbols and messages on the stones were marking the exact locations of wormholes here on earth, where the shortcuts would appear."

"It was just rotten luck," I said, "that Anna, and then you, were standing in that spot when the wormhole opened."

Léon turned around and pointed ahead, down the trail.

We were back at the pillars.

There had been so much happening when we arrived the day before, I never really had a chance to examine the markers. They were the exact same stones, of course, but they looked slightly different. Some of the carvings appeared newer, fresher, and some of the glyphs had less moss and lichen growth.

Thank goodness. We made it, I thought.

Eric went straight to the centre of the three stones

and threw down his bag. "Good. So who wants to go first?"

"Ladies first?" I asked Rachel, tossing my backpack on the ground next to Eric's. I dug out a water bottle and passed it around.

"Do you think it could carry all of us at once?" Eric said. "Or are we too heavy?"

Anna took a drink of water and gave the bottle to Eric. "I do not think it works like an elevator," she said wryly.

Eric frowned. "I'm just worried that the meteor shower won't last long enough to transport all of us."

"Yeah, you've got a point," I agreed. "But we do know that two people can pass through the wormhole at the same time. So why don't Anna and Rachel go first, and then we'll jump in as soon as they vanish."

Anna and Rachel nodded. It seemed like a good plan. The girls stood in the centre, back-to-back and holding hands, waiting to disappear.

Eric paced in a circle around the girls. "It should happen any second now."

Anna and Rachel shook with nervous energy.

I picked up my pack and swung it on my back

again. "We'll see you on the other side," I said, trying hard to sound optimistic.

Eric strapped his bag on too. "Any second now . . . "

"Stop saying that!" Rachel snapped. "I'm nervous enough as it is."

Minutes passed, but nothing happened. Eric stopped doing laps around Anna and Rachel. "Something's not right," he mumbled.

"Give it time," I said. "Don't move now. Stay put." But even as I said that, I wondered if Eric was right.

"Why are we still here?" Rachel asked, staring angrily at the sky.

We didn't know the answer to that, so we didn't say anything.

Léon, who had been standing several feet back from the centre of the pillars, shook his head. "It seems you are destined to stay here," he said, sounding far too smug.

"But how could that be?" I asked. "We're doing everything exactly the same."

Anna and Rachel refused to give up and stubbornly stayed in the centre of the stones.

Eric unstrapped his pack and threw it on the grass. "So now what?" he griped, to nobody in particular.

"Are we stuck here forever?"

"This is crazy," I said. "We're doing the same thing we did to get here. It should have worked."

"Unless we have missed the entire astronomical event," Anna said, letting go of Rachel and moving away from her. "Perhaps we are days or weeks too late."

Rachel looked stricken. "What does that mean? You mean we'll have to wait until next summer to go home?"

I nodded. "Unless we can interpret Gaelic, or Chinese, or Mayan. Then maybe we can bounce to some other petroform site. There's a chance those wormholes might get us back to the cemetery in Sultana."

Rachel looked down at her feet. "I have a bad feeling we're going to be stuck here for another year."

CHAPTER
8

WE HAD LOITERED near the petroform all day, taking turns sitting in the centre and waiting for the wormhole to take us home. Nothing happened, of course, and now it was late afternoon. Anna and Rachel were stretched out in the shade talking softly, Eric was napping in the centre of the stones, and I was wandering aimlessly around the site, worrying if we'd ever make it back to our time.

Léon had left right after our failed attempt to use the time portal, explaining that he needed to update the chief. And as I'd watched him leave, I remembered how satisfied he seemed when the wormhole didn't open. Maybe he knew we couldn't leave, I now wondered, because he had tried to leave years ago. But then, why wouldn't he tell us that?

After kicking the nearest pillar in frustration

(ouch!), I stomped over to the next stone. While trying to shake my foul mood, I also began to notice the sun dipping behind the tall spruce trees to the northwest.

The northwest?

The northwest?

I stopped walking and studied the path the sun was taking down to the horizon. Hmmm. I tried to imagine the layout of the cemetery and the location of my house back in Sultana. Something suddenly seemed off . . . different.

That's it!

The sun was going to set way more to the north today. Back home, the sun would be setting due west. And that meant—I closed my eyes to concentrate—we arrived here at least a month earlier in the summer. Which meant . . .

Oh, no! No! No! No!

The significance suddenly sunk in. If we arrived here in June, and the meteor showers weren't due until August . . . We were stuck here for another month!

My head began to swim with panic, and I felt like I was going to pass out. I had to sit down. Then I realized my legs had collapsed, and I was already sitting down. I took three deep breaths, closed my eyes and reconsidered my findings. I was hoping I was wrong about the time of year, but after reviewing all the facts again and again, I knew I wasn't. It was June.

I stood up slowly and began walking over to the girls. I was about to give them some very bad news.

But there must be a way to get out of here, I thought. The ancients travelled back and forth along the timeline—at least, that's what Bruno said—so there was no reason why we couldn't do that too. Those people even took the trouble to mark the wormhole locations and provide written instructions and . . .

"That's it!" I whispered to myself. I changed course and hustled back to the nearest pillar. I examined the symbols that I thought were left by Native North Americans, and as I suspected, they were exactly the same as the symbols on the stones in the cemetery. I mean, they had to be, right? They were the same stones. Sure, the messages looked slightly different, because they were newer and less weathered. But other than that, I was looking at the same pillar . . .

Huh?

I squinted at the base of the stone, suddenly seeing something new—a series of engravings not visible in Sultana.

Anna and Rachel walked over to join me. "Did you find something, Cody?" Anna asked.

I quickly forgot about the bad news and focused on this new opportunity to get us home. "Yeah," I said, pointing at the pillar, just above the grass and earth. "I don't remember this message being on our stones, in the cemetery."

Anna stood and compared the height of the rock with her body. "I think you are right," she said. "More of this rock is visible and exposed."

Rachel dropped to her knees and examined the symbols. "The soil must have built up slowly over the decades, hiding more and more of the rock—and this message."

I had another thought and quickly shared it. "What if," I began, "we weren't able to travel back, because we never read the right instructions to get back."

"What do you mean?" Rachel said.

"Well, what if these pillars here—actually, all the

pillars—are kind of like the departure boards at an airport? Those boards tell you when and from where your plane leaves. Right?"

The girls nodded.

"Well, we just assumed that we could leave this time period the same way we left our time. But that didn't work, because we never checked the departure board—or rather, the pillars—for our instructions." I pointed at the newly discovered message at the bottom of the stone.

Anna and Rachel looked at each other like I was talking gibberish.

So I clarified my gibberish. "We can't just walk into an airport, hop on any old plane, and expect to end up where we want to end up. We have to read the instructions on the departure boards and then go to the correct gate at a specific time to end up in the right place."

Rachel started nodding slowly. "I think you're onto something."

"Do you have a pen or pencil?" Anna asked, getting excited. "I will sketch these messages and patterns so we can look at them later."

I found a pencil and some paper in my backpack.

Then Rachel and I watched as Anna skillfully copied the symbols and messages left so long ago. She was just as good an artist as Rachel.

Rachel smiled for the first time in hours. "So if we can figure out this new set of instructions, we might still be able to get out of here."

"Exactly," I said. "We need to—"

I broke off when I heard people coming down the trail, from the direction of the Cree camp. It was Léon and the three kids we had helped that morning. The children kept their distance from the lanky adult. I didn't blame them.

Now what? I wondered.

Léon walked up to us and said, "Zee chief 'as asked me to escort you back to zee camp. 'e fears for your safety if you stay in zee forest overnight." Maybe I was being paranoid again, but he said that like he couldn't have cared less about our safety.

I looked around the clearing. The area looked pretty harmless to me, and since I'd already spent a night in the bush, I wasn't too worried about it. Plus, we needed to figure out the meaning of those symbols as soon as possible. We had to make as much use of the fading light as we could.

I opened my mouth, about to tell Léon to "buzz off and leave us alone," when one of the kids mumbled something in Cree. The boy shifted from foot to foot and looked about nervously.

"What did he say?" Anna asked.

All the talking woke Eric, and he meandered over to join us. The kids gave him a sly smile and secret nod that Léon didn't see. I had been worried that they would rat on us, but after seeing those smiles, I doubted it.

Léon explained their presence.

"Barks-Like-An-Otter," Léon pointed at the little girl who had almost died that morning, "insisted zat she and 'er friends come with me to make sure you come back to zee camp. She said you must return to zee camp so zat you will be safe from Windigo."

"Who," I asked, "or what is that?"

"It is a silly story zat zee kids believe. I'm sure you will learn about 'im sometime."

"I don't think I want to meet him," Eric said, clearly stalling. "Look at how he's freaking out the kids."

Léon frowned down at Eric.

"Zat is not what I meant. In zee evenings we tell stories at camp. Zere might be one about Windigo.

Don't worry. Now you 'ave plenty of time to learn all our stories."

I scowled. I didn't like what he was implying.

The children must have sensed our reluctance, because Barks-Like-An-Otter started yanking on Eric's arm, pulling him back toward camp.

Eric laughed. "Hey, Cody, I think we've made friends for life."

Anna and Rachel looked at each other with confused expressions. In our hurry to make it to the stones, we had forgotten to tell them about the near-drowning. But I sure wasn't going to say anything now, in front of Léon. If he could keep secrets, so could we.

"A group of men from zee camp has not yet returned from a trading trip downriver," Léon said. "Some of zee women 'ave agreed to move to other tents, so zat you may 'ave a teepee to yourselves."

"Isn't the tribe worried about them? Because of that creature you warned us about?"

Léon shook his head. "Windigo is a part of Cree folklore—zat is all. Zey are stories told to frighten children." He pointed at the jittery kids with a long bony finger, as if to prove his point.

"It might be nice for all of us to be together and get a proper night's sleep," Rachel said.

"And it will be dark in a few hours," Anna added.

Léon looked up at the sky. "We should go. It is mealtime."

"That settles it," Eric said. "If it's suppertime, let's go. I'm sick of granola bars and water. I need some home-cooking."

I reluctantly agreed. If there really was safety in numbers—that's what adults always said—we might be better off back at camp. And we could figure out the rest—Léon, the chief, and the pillars—in comfort.

We grabbed our packs and followed Léon and the kids back to their campsite. Barks-Like-An-Otter skipped along beside Eric and chattered non-stop with her little pals. They made enough noise so that I could stay back and tell Anna and Rachel about the drowning without fear of being overheard.

"I can't believe I'm going to say this," Rachel said, "but thank goodness Eric had to pee. Otherwise . . ."

"That explains why they were so eager to have us return to the camp," Anna said. "They wanted to return the kindness you showed them. And a way for them to do that is to keep you safe from the forest monsters. They might be mythical to us, but they are obviously real to them."

We knew it was dinnertime when we got to the camp because the smell of food rose to the sky like billows of smoke. As expected, Eric's gut rumbled and grumbled. A string of fresh fish was cooking over the main firepit near the centre of the camp. Another lady was making some sort of bread, and a huge pot of wild rice sat steaming next to her.

We all froze and stared wide-eyed at the feast being prepared all around us. We hadn't eaten any real food for a long time and we were starving. The Cree women who were assembling supper saw us gawking and waved us over to join them. They laughed and said something to Léon.

Léon translated. "Zey said you should all eat as much as you can. Zey are joking zat perhaps no one wants you back because you look 'alf-dead."

I had to laugh too. I suppose we did look like four unhealthy kids, especially Eric and Rachel with their blond hair and lighter complexions. To the Cree, they probably looked like walking corpses.

Somehow word had spread quickly through the

camp that we were back from the stones and that we weren't going anywhere. People poured out of teepees and gathered around the food—more food than I'd ever seen in once place. In fact, it dawned on me that this was a welcome-to-the-family dinner. And that was too bad, because I still planned on getting home.

Léon gave us each a wooden bowl and wandered off. I started off my supper with a huge scoop of wild rice. I saw a few rice husks, but otherwise it looked exactly like the wild rice my mom made. And it tasted just as good. I was nervous that the meat—deer or moose or caribou—would taste gross and gamey like the stuff Uncle Mitch dragged out of the freezer when we visited him. But it was cooked perfectly. They didn't use—or have—as many spices as we did, but all the meats were tender and flavourful.

When we finished mopping our bowls with bannock, Barks-Like-An-Otter spoiled Eric and me with fresh blueberries and strawberries. Eric didn't seem to mind all the extra attention.

"It must be nice for you guys, having your own personal server," Rachel teased.

I laughed and popped another strawberry in my mouth. "It's not our fault we're heroes."

Eric nodded. "Saving people is what I was born to do—just like Indiana Jones."

"If only I could remember all this," he continued, "I'd get an awesome grade next year in Canadian History."

"Yeah," Rachel agreed, "this is pretty amazing. We're actually spending time with the first people in Canada. And a real voyageur."

Eric scowled at the chief over his bowl of fruit. "Too bad he smashed your camera. It would be neat to get some pictures of him and—"

"Are you kidding?" I said. "We can't start taking pictures of the chief with a digital camera. What would we do with the photos? I mean, we can't go back to school and do a presentation on 'How We Time-Travelled and Met a Real Cree Chief.'"

We all laughed and then looked at Chief Raven-Feather—Léon had told us his name. The chief was eating with our group, but Léon was farther away with another cluster of diners. I noticed the chief's fingers had lots of small cuts on them from demonstrating to everyone how sharp his new knife was.

The chief yelled for Léon to come over. He stood up without much enthusiasm, ambled over to where we were eating and sat down with us. The chief said something, and we waited for Léon to translate. "Zee chief suggests you show your appreciation for zee meal by presenting 'im with another gift."

We looked at each other in disbelief.

The chief started laughing like a madman and slapped Léon on the back so hard he almost rolled over onto some leftover fish fillets.

When Léon recovered his composure, he said, "Zee chief said 'e is only joking with you, and zat you all need to relax and not be so serious."

What a character!

"Tell us your story," Eric said to Léon. "How did you come to be here?"

Léon nodded, like he was expecting one of us to ask that.

"I was born," he said, "in 1766 in a small town called Montréal. Perhaps you 'ave heard of it?"

"It's not so small anymore," Eric said.

"Ahh, so it is prospering?"

We all murmured that it was.

"When I was sixteen," he continued, "I signed on with zee Hudson's Bay Company as a voyageur. Zee work was terribly 'ard. Long days. Paddling.

Paddling. Paddling. Sleeping in zee cold . . . " His eyes glazed over with a distant look.

"That does sound rough," I said.

Léon blinked himself back to the story. "Anyway, after twelve weeks I 'ad enough. I wanted to quit. But 'ow could I leave? I was in zee middle of North America. Zen, one evening after we 'ad set up camp, I went to explore zee area. I found some interesting rocks with writing on zem, and zee next zing I knew I was somewhere else. It was all very confusing for me."

"Tell me about it," Eric said.

Léon ignored that and said, "I wandered for days, looking for my men—my fellow voyageurs. I zought zey left me behind and . . . and I was 'appy. Very 'appy. Zen zee Cree found me and welcomed me. I 'ad a new family."

"Did you know you travelled back in time?" Rachel asked.

"As zee years passed, and as I learned zee Cree language, I began to understand—and to believe—zat zat was what 'ad 'appened. I do not care if it was magic, or God, or something else zat brought me 'ere, but my life is better now."

"Don't you miss your old world?" Eric asked.

"*Non*. I only miss my little sister, Elyse." He looked at Rachel and smiled, and then gave Eric and me a hard look. "But zis is my 'ome now and I would not want anything to change for my people." He stood and walked away.

After everyone had eaten their fill, all the band members pitched in and quickly cleaned up. The cooking utensils were gathered and washed on the banks of the river. And the uneaten food was carefully packaged and placed in a deep hole on the eastern edge of the camp. I suppose without a refrigerator, the best way to keep stuff cool was to put it in the ground. If all that smoked meat was stored in the tents, it would definitely attract bears. They were doing everything we were taught to do in Boy Scouts, only they were never taught to do it. They just knew.

We watched Léon help one of the women place a heavy stone on the cover of the food storage locker. We had a few minutes to talk before he'd be back.

"Anna has an idea—a really good idea," Rachel said.

"Oh yeah," I asked, "what is it?"

Anna turned around to make sure Léon wasn't

coming back. "Well," she said, "what if we ignored the symbols and glyphs from all the cultures, and focused on the ones we know are from North American Natives? Perhaps the chief or one of the Elders could make sense of those figures."

Rachel pulled out the paper and pointed to the cluster of glyphs Anna had copied from the base of the stones. Three small shapes formed a triangle and clearly represented the stones—that was a no-brainer. But the other symbols were more obscure. There was a circle with a line underneath it, a crazy lightning bolt thingy, and an object I could best describe as a comb.

Eric took a quick look at it too, before Rachel slipped it into her bag again. "Maybe," he suggested, "someone here can look in a Cree book and tell us what it all means."

Anna shook her head. "That's not possible. They have oral traditions."

"What does that mean?" Eric asked.

"Well, the ancient Egyptians, for example, documented everything," Anna said. "They wrote down even the most boring day-to-day things. But the early Cree passed on all their legends and myths and ancestry through stories told orally—not through books."

Eric frowned. "But if we can't find a scribe here, how can we get your sketches translated?"

Anna nodded. "The symbols themselves still have meaning. Everything we see around camp has been adorned with symbols and patterns and artwork. To us it may only look like decoration, but I suspect every design holds messages too."

"I still don't get it," Eric said.

Anna was patient and tried to explain. "If I took a piece of paper and painted an eye, a heart shape, and a horseshoe, does that mean anything to you?"

"Sure," Eric said, "I see that all the time. It means, 'I . . . love . . . you.'"

"Exactly," Anna said. "I did not use the English alphabet to spell that out—I used symbols—but you still understood the message. The Cree would not understand those 'I love you' symbols, just as we cannot understand their symbols. But still, even without a written alphabet, they are using symbols to communicate."

We all looked around the camp. Anna was absolutely right. Everything was decorated—the tents, the weapons, the food bowls, the clothing. I felt a new hope grow inside me. Someone—perhaps one of the Elders—had to know what the symbols on the pillars meant.

The sun slipped below the horizon. One of the men threw heaps of wood onto the coals that had cooked our food. The dry logs quickly ignited, and the heat pushed us back several feet. The children in the camp who had been eating their supper with their family members gathered around an old man. Older kids made a semi-circle behind the little kids, and the rest of the adults stayed back, forming a perimeter.

The chief bellowed something to Léon and then pointed at us. Léon grimaced, but reluctantly came over and sat down next to Rachel. He seemed to like her more than the rest of us. "I am to translate," was all he said.

"Is he the storyteller?" Rachel asked.

"*Oui*," Léon said. "'e is our entertainer, our story-teller, and our 'istorian. 'is name is Ghost-Keeper."

I felt an elbow jab me. "Now, that's a guy we want to talk to," Eric whispered. "If he's the historian, he has to know about their symbols—it's his job."

Rachel heard what Eric said, so she elbowed him. "If we're going to ask for his help later, you better show him some respect now."

Once the kids had settled down, he began telling stories. We couldn't understand anything Ghost-Keeper said, but it was just as entertaining to watch him. He didn't just talk, he acted out whatever he was trying to say. He stood up, he sat down, and he even leapt into the air one time, as spry and nimble as a cricket, provoking sharp screams from some of the kids. And me too—I actually jumped when he did that.

"He's terrific," Rachel said quietly.

"What is that story about?" Anna asked Léon. "It looks very interesting."

"'e always begins with zis story," Léon explained. "It is called Turtles Never Run. Zee children love it."

Everyone broke into laughter when his tale ended. The children implored Ghost-Keeper to continue. He pretended to be exhausted. Standing up, he faked a great yawn and suggested he was going to leave and go to sleep. But the kids wouldn't have any of that. They whined and they begged, and after a minute, he sat down again with an exaggerated sigh.

The storyteller saw us grinning and waved us even closer, inviting us to be part of his audience. Ghost-Keeper said something to Léon, and Léon translated. "Next, 'e will tell zee story Why Beaver Has a Flat Tail."

Léon nodded, and the Elder began again.

"Many moons ago, Beaver 'ad a long, thin tail. And 'is neighbour, Muskrat, 'ad a big, fat, flat tail. Beaver loved zee sound Muskrat's tail made when it 'it zee water."

Ghost-Keeper slapped his hands to mimic the sound of a beaver smacking his tail against the water. The sudden smacking sound made the kids, including me (again), jump.

"Beaver became jealous of Muskrat's beautiful tail. 'e thought about 'ow much fun 'e could have if only 'e 'ad a tail like zat. 'e could show it to all 'is friends, and zey would be impressed with zee thunderous clap it made—if only it was 'is."

The kids around me were all grinning. I realized that to them, this was like when Eric and I laughed at a cartoon on TV, even though we'd already seen it ten times.

"Beaver couldn't eat, or sleep, or work on 'is dam. All 'e did was think about Muskrat's tail and 'ow 'e wanted it. So one day, 'e asked Muskrat if zey could trade tails for one day—just one day. Muskrat said no, but Beaver would not give up. Every day 'e pestered Muskrat to trade with 'im. Finally, Muskrat 'ad 'ad enough, and 'e agreed to swap tails with Beaver for a day. But the following morning, when Muskrat asked for 'is flat tail back, Beaver shook 'is 'ead."

The open-mouthed children shook their heads too, displaying their disappointment with Beaver's sneaky trick.

"Muskrat screamed and begged for 'is tail, but Beaver ignored 'im and vanished into a bog. And to zis day, Beaver 'as not returned Muskrat's tail."

When Ghost-Keeper finished, I saw a lot of the adults offering satisfied nods. The stories are often different, I thought, but the message to kids is the same—be happy with what you have.

The storyteller pointed at the open space next to him. Then, he pointed at me.

Oh, no. Now what?

CHAPTER 9

ERIC LAUGHED AND pushed me toward Ghost-Keeper.

I groaned inwardly and snaked my way toward the storyteller. When I was standing next to him, with my back to the fire, he said something to Léon.

"'e asks zat you share a story now," Léon explained, enjoying my discomfort. "To refuse would be an insult."

Oh brother.

Anna nodded her encouragement, and Rachel winked at me and said, "Go ahead, Cody, tell us a story."

"And make it a good one," Eric added. "Or I'm going to fall asleep."

Of course, I could have declined. I could have pretended I had a sore throat, or a ruptured appendix, or something. But we needed his help, and I wanted to go back home, so I took a deep breath and decided to wing it.

"This story," I began, "is called . . . ahh . . . Never Believe a Fox. Many moons ago, Handsome Fox and Hungry Fox were playing near their home. They loved their forest and their river, but as they played, they began to fear that they may have to move soon, because there were too few mice left for them to eat. So Handsome Fox and Hungry Fox came up with a plan—they would trick the mice to come to them. They just didn't know how to trick the mice."

The kids laughed politely as Léon translated. Maybe this wasn't so bad.

"Handsome Fox and Hungry Fox were not very smart, so they asked Clever Fox for her advice. Clever Fox considered the problem and told Handsome Fox and Hungry Fox what to do. They left their home and went into the forest, where they told all the animals that they were tired of eating seeds and wild rice and wild oats and all the things mice love. They explained that to the north—that was where Handsome Fox and Hungry Fox lived—there was so much mouse food, they had to leave and go south to find fox food."

The children grinned and leaned forward, eager for me to continue. Some of the adults chatting quietly at the back stopped talking and listened to Léon's translations. Happy no one was falling asleep, I continued with more confidence.

"Word spread quickly among the mice that there was a land of plenty to the north—a place free of mouse-eaters and with lots of food. Handsome Fox and Hungry Fox snuck back home and waited excitedly. The mice soon followed. Their plan was working perfectly, and they feasted on mice all day long. But the mice kept coming—more mice than they could eat. Handsome Fox grew monstrously fat—"

I puffed up my cheeks and pretended I had a belly like Santa Claus. Everyone laughed as Léon turned my story into Cree.

"And Hungry Fox was weary of eating mice and longed for the taste of a frog or a bird. Their plan had worked too well. Finally, they had had enough. They told the mice it was just a trick, and that there was no extra mouse food. Word of the trick swept through the forest and reached all the mice. And they all left as quickly as they came. Handsome Fox and Hungry Fox didn't have to move from their home, but they did have to work harder and harder to catch their food."

I waited for Léon to translate what I said, and then I wrapped up my story. "So foxes are sly and sneaky, and you should never trust one. The end."

Ghost-Keeper stood up—he'd been sitting on a log—and put a hand on my shoulder. He said something loudly in Cree. Léon explained what the storyteller had said. "'e will remember zat story and tell it in zee future. 'e also said zat you may become 'is . . . apprentice storyteller."

In that instant, it dawned on me that they expected us to stay with them forever—to be part of their family. Yikes!

I bowed politely and then quickly walked back to stand beside Eric. I didn't want to be cajoled into another tale.

"That was pretty lame," Eric said, giggling.

"It wasn't lame at all, Handsome Fox," Rachel said.

"Huh?" Eric looked puzzled.

Rachel laughed and looked at her brother. "That story didn't sound familiar to you, Hungry Fox?"

"No," Eric said. "Wait. That was about us?"

Rachel shook her head.

"At least you didn't offend Ghost-Keeper." Eric indicated the storyteller with his chin. "We need to keep him on our good side."

"Yeah," I said, "maybe we can visit with him first thing in the morning."

We told Léon we were exhausted and excused ourselves to go to the tent assigned to us. He looked at us suspiciously, but didn't stop us. For a guy who said he'd help us, he was trying awfully hard to keep an eye on us.

Our tent was very cozy. One of the Cree women had lit three homemade candles and placed them on the stones that formed the firepit in the centre. The candles were smelly and the smoke tickled my nose, but the flames gave the inside of the teepee a nice glow. We made ourselves comfortable on the furs that covered the ground.

Rachel took the paper from her backpack and passed around the sketch Anna had made. There was just enough light to examine the symbols.

"These symbols look a lot like the ones on the stones in the cemetery," I said, pointing at the characters. "But I think there's something different about them as well."

"I did not have time to draw all the messages," Anna said apologetically. "Only the ones Cody found near the bottom."

"Too bad the chief had to go and smash Rachel's camera," Eric said again. He put a stack of small furs under his head to make a pillow. "I'm pretty sure she took a picture of the other symbols in Sultana."

"Yeah, I did," Rachel said. "It would have been nice to compare the exposed glyphs with these." She pointed at the sketches Anna was now holding.

Anna stared at the page for a long time without blinking. "Wait a minute!" she cried. Anna dropped the paper on Eric's chest, jumped up and ran from the teepee.

"What's she up to?" I asked.

Eric shrugged. "Maybe she has to pee really badly."

I sighed and closed my eyes. I was glad we had returned to the camp. I felt safer with the Cree watching over us. With all their bush skills and survival know-how, we were definitely in their Sultana now—on their turf.

We continued to settle down for the night while we waited for Anna to come back.

Ten minutes later, we started to worry Anna had

gotten lost. But then the tent flap flew open and she stormed inside, huffing and excited.

"Maybe we can still use this," Anna said. She sat down and proudly held out the small memory card from the camera. The chief had destroyed Rachel's birthday present, but the memory card looked intact.

"No way!" Eric said, sitting up again. "How on earth did you find that?"

Anna grinned, pleased with her discovery. "It is dark outside, but I remembered where we had left the camera, and I looked through the broken pieces. Do you have a second camera?"

The three of us shook our heads.

"Oh," Anna said, deflated. "Do any of you have a smart phone?"

Rachel shook her head. But Eric and I didn't.

"Yes, we do," Eric said. "Your dad gave us his." Eric dug it out of the backpack and passed it to Anna.

"I am sure Papa's phone uses a memory card like this," she said, quickly removing the protective cover and back panel. Seconds later, she proudly held up the phone's tiny memory card. "It is the same!" She swapped cards, opened the directory with the photographs and passed the phone to Rachel.

"I sure hope the card's not damaged," Rachel said.

We gathered around the phone and watched as Rachel flipped through the photos.

Anna sighed. "I am so sorry that Papa got you involved in this . . . in this mess. But I am still glad you all came to help me."

"It's a lucky thing we broke the law," Eric said, "otherwise we never would have been in that graveyard, at that time." He quickly described the fake tablet we had made, and our punishment for that misadventure.

"Very clever." Anna said. "And very creative."

Rachel continued to flick her way through the pictures until she found the ones from the stones in Sultana.

"Stop!" I said. "That's it." She zoomed in so that the whole message filled the LCD screen.

Eric twisted the device so that he could see it better. "So if Cody is right, one set of instructions got us here, and the other set of instructions—the one Anna copied—might take us home again."

Anna held her piece of paper next to the display. "I believe the difference is in these symbols here." She tapped the glyphs on the left side.

"Maybe we can work backwards," Rachel suggested, "using the information we already know to be true."

"Good," Eric said. "Let's try that."

"All right," I said. "So here's what we know. We travelled to this world because we were all standing in a wormhole when it opened. And that happened to coincide with the Perseid meteor shower."

Everyone nodded.

"This symbol here," Eric said, pointing at the screen, "has to be the symbol they used for the sky."

"Yes," Anna agreed. "See how it has spots coming from it."

"For sure," I said. "Those must represent the meteor shower."

"Okay. So now that we know the message," Rachel said, "the symbols on the stones seem pretty logical. They've got everything included here—the pillars, the earth, and the actual meteor shower."

"That was the puzzle your dad solved," I said to Anna.

Eric poked Anna's drawing. "But what about this stuff? There are two or three symbols at the base of the pillars that we don't see in the other message."

Anna said, "Both messages originate from the

same culture—Native North American—and use the same logic. So it should not be too difficult to interpret their meaning."

Two of the candles in our teepee flickered and then burned out. The light was fading fast. We didn't want to start using the flashlight, so we decided to wait until the morning to decipher the rest of the symbols. Plus, we could barely keep our eyes open.

"Tomorrow," I said, "we can ask Ghost-Keeper and the other Elders if they have any ideas about these figures."

Anna blew out the last candle, and we all stretched out around the cold firepit in the centre of the tent. We fell asleep to the peaceful night sounds of the wilderness around us.

Only I didn't fall asleep right away.

As I listened to the wind in the trees outside and the call of a distant loon, a thought began to trouble me. I wasn't sure what my tired brain was getting at, but it was gently trying to help me remember something—something I had seen . . .

CHAPTER 10

THE FOLLOWING MORNING I was roughly shaken awake.

I opened my eyes to find Barks-Like-An-Otter shoving me enthusiastically. She tugged on my arm until I sat up—my commitment to her that I wouldn't go to sleep again. I looked around the tent for the girls, but they were already gone. I rubbed my eyes and watched as Eric received the same wake-up call. She pushed and pulled on his shoulders until he too gave up. When we were both sitting upright, Barks-Like-An-Otter indicated—by pretending to shovel something in her mouth—that we should join her for breakfast.

"I suppose if I'm not allowed to sleep," Eric said, "I may as well eat."

Summer-Blessing—that's Barks-Like-An-Otter's

mother—was waiting for us outside the tent. She waved for us to follow her and join her and the girls for breakfast—fresh bannock with honey and mashed berries. It tasted better than any pancake I'd ever had back home.

Anna and Rachel had already eaten and were now keenly studying the paper with the sketches. Rachel took the page, passed it to Summer-Blessing, and tapped the glyphs. Summer-Blessing said something in Cree, shook her head and looked around the camp. She spotted Léon speaking with the chief and pointed to him.

"I guess she can't help us either," I said.

Rachel stood up and took the page to an Elder who was trying to patch one of the birch bark canoes. He stopped dripping pine tar on the crack and smiled at Rachel. I watched closely as the man examined the sketch and then, just like Summer-Blessing, pointed at Léon.

Rachel took Anna's drawing to three other Cree and got similar reactions—shrugs, head shakes, and gestures toward Léon.

This was getting more and more suspicious.

Rachel joined us again several minutes later.

"No one knows anything," she said, passing Anna the paper.

"Hmmm," I said.

Eric put down the piece of bannock he was just about to pop into his mouth. "What's up?" he asked.

"I think they know a lot," I said. "They just don't know how to tell us what they know."

"What do you mean?" Rachel asked.

I checked to make sure Léon still had his back to us, then I poked Summer-Blessing on the shoulder to get her attention. When she looked at me, I traced the intricate painted design on her teepee with my finger. Then I pointed at her.

She understood what I was asking and shook her head. No, I did not paint the teepee.

I lifted my shoulders and made my eyes big. Who did draw this?

She looked around the camp and pointed at Léon.

"Oh!" Eric said.

"What do you mean, 'Oh?'" Anna asked.

"I think that Léon knows what all the symbols mean," I said, "but he doesn't want to tell us."

"But why would he not tell us what he knows?" Anna asked.

"Maybe he's lonely," Eric suggested.

"Maybe he misses speaking English and French," I said, staring at Léon.

"Or maybe," Eric rambled on, "he's afraid that if we leave, we'll rat on him. Maybe he thinks some voyageur is going to come here and haul him back to his hard life paddling the rivers."

"That's silly," Rachel said. "Plus, we know adults can't use the wormhole."

"We know that," Eric said, "but does Léon?"

Everyone was quiet for a few minutes as we considered Léon's motivations. He was still chatting with the chief at the far end of the camp, and I was still watching them both. "You know," I said, "the truth might be even simpler than that."

"What are you thinking?" Eric asked.

"Maybe he just doesn't want anyone to mess with the Cree—his adoptive family." I said. "If I were him, I wouldn't want to risk other people showing up and exploiting the Cree."

Anna nodded. "Perhaps he also feels some guilt for the way the fur traders treated the Cree."

"The bottom line is," Eric said, "it's pretty rotten of him to keep four kids trapped here against their will."

"Let's just forget about Léon for now," I said, "and get back to the real puzzle—those new symbols on the stones." I pointed at the paper Anna was holding.

"We all agree that we can't trust him—for whatever reason—so let's just decipher this message and get the heck out of here."

"Yeah," Eric said. "We're on our own."

Anna stared fixedly at the drawing on her lap. "When Rachel showed the other Cree my drawing, they all shook their heads—like they did not know anything. So where do we start?"

"I think they shook their heads because they can't speak English," I said. "But they all pointed to Léon. And that's either because he speaks English, or because he's the artist who painted all this stuff."

"Maybe . . . " Rachel said. "But could he really have learned all their symbols since arriving here?"

"Hmmm . . . " Anna said, contemplating the question. "It is possible. A fast learner could easily memorize the meaning of one or two hundred glyphs."

"Bits and pieces of the images we need to interpret have probably been painted on most of these teepees," I said. "If you look carefully, you'll find that someone has been using similar symbols and glyphs as artwork for years." That was what was bothering me last night. Some of the symbols on the pillars were almost identical to the decorations on the tents!

"We're getting real close to figuring this thing out," Eric mumbled, "and I bet he's getting nervous about it."

Our heads automatically turned towards Léon.

Anna took a deep breath and slowly let it out. "But if we cannot ask Léon for his help, what are we going to do?"

"We need to keep acting like nothing's wrong," Rachel said.

"Yeah," Eric agreed, "or else he might really mess up our chance of escaping from this place."

I nodded. "But at the same time we have to work quickly to figure out what those unknown symbols mean. I'd hate to find out tomorrow that whatever event we're waiting for has already passed."

"What could it be?" Anna wondered out loud.

"Who knows?" I said, looking at Anna's drawing for the hundredth time. "It could be a comet, an eclipse, a thunderstorm . . . anything."

"I just hope we haven't missed it," Eric said. "I don't

mind camping here for a few days, but I sure don't want to live here forever."

"You do live here, silly," Rachel said, trying to lighten the mood. "Remember, this is Sultana."

Eric snorted. "You know what I mean."

We helped Summer-Blessing clean up after breakfast, and then lent a hand with some camp chores. After we were done, we put our plan into action. It was simple: Rachel would distract Léon by pretending to want to learn Cree, while Anna, Eric, and I quizzed the Elders and Ghost-Keeper about the symbols.

Rachel persuaded Léon to go for a walk to the stones. She told him she wanted to learn the Cree words for everything they saw along the way. Once they were on the trail and out of sight, we went to work.

Anna took her sketch and headed off to find the chief, while Eric and I searched for Ghost-Keeper. We found him making arrowheads behind one of the tents. He looked up at us, smiled and kept working the stone. He finished scratching something onto the arrowhead and handed it to me. I looked at the piece of flint and studied it closely.

"Look," I said pointing at the head, "he carved a feather onto the side."

"Cool!" Eric said, taking the arrowhead. "Maybe that's like his stamp or seal, so if anyone finds the arrow they'll know it's his." He tried to pass the arrowhead back, but Ghost-Keeper indicated it was ours to keep.

We nodded our thanks.

I showed him a sketch I had made, a drawing on a piece of birch bark with some charcoal. He seemed delighted, probably because he thought I was preparing for my training as his apprentice. That made me feel kind of guilty. He looked at the white bark, said something in Cree and stared at the sky. I thought he might be saying a prayer, but then I realized he was waiting for a cloud to slide away. When the sun finally poked out again, Ghost-Keeper pointed up at it with another slab of flint.

"So far so good," Eric said.

"Now let's try the other symbols." I took a blackened stick and drew one of the unknown glyphs. I could have shown him the whole series of images at once, but I was afraid it might be confusing.

Ghost-Keeper waited patiently for me to finish

it. He seemed in no hurry to get back to work. When I was done, he took the birch bark again and examined it.

He reached over and snapped a two-foot-long branch off a poplar tree. Then he shoved the stick into the dirt. He drew a circle around the base and pointed at the sliver of a shadow cast by the sun over the stick.

"I don't get it," Eric said.

I shrugged, letting Ghost-Keeper know how slow we were.

He held his fist directly over the stick and pointed at the sun.

"Oh, no!" I groaned.

"What?" Eric asked.

My heart began to race. "I think he's indicating the summer solstice, when the sun is at . . . at its highest."

Eric shook his head. "But that was last month."

"It was last month in our world," I said, "but we arrived here earlier in the summer."

Eric didn't look convinced. "Are you sure about that?"

I explained my sunset observations from last night.

Eric began nodding. "Yeah, that makes sense. It does seem like we have more hours of daylight again."

I pointed at the stick and the sun high above us. "Today?" I asked. "Now?" I knew Ghost-Keeper didn't understand English, but I was frantic.

He nodded.

"I don't know . . . " Eric said. "He could be saying yes to anything—an egg, a shooting star, a bird."

The storyteller smoothed the dirt around the stick and showed me again how short the shadow was.

"Okay," Eric admitted, "that does seem like a noontime shadow."

Just then, Anna ran around the corner and came hurtling at us. "It is today!" she screamed. "The cosmic event is today!" She paused and tried to catch her breath.

Ghost-Keeper, startled by Anna's sudden arrival, dropped the carving tool he had been holding. He ignored the fallen stone and gave Anna a welcoming grin. At least he liked kids.

"Is it the solstice?" I asked, looking for confirmation.

"Yes," she said. "It is the summer solstice."

Anna went on to explain that the chief had agreed

that the series of symbols represented the summer solstice—the longest day of the year.

Ghost-Keeper was still watching us with interest, but didn't say anything. I felt a twinge of regret that I couldn't stay and be his apprentice. He was a pretty cool guy.

"It all makes sense now," I said. "If the people who used the wormhole made accurate calculations, the wormhole on this end will begin to close when the days start getting shorter, right after the solstice."

Eric added, "So maybe we can still make it out of here."

"We must make it out of here today," Anna said. "We will not get a second chance tomorrow."

"We need to find Rachel," I said, "and get to the pillars." I pulled my wristwatch from my pocket and studied the dials. "My guess is we've got about an hour before the solstice."

My heart was pounding so loudly I could hardly think straight. We needed to move!

"Let's get the backpacks," Eric said, "and head for the stones."

Suddenly we heard a commotion by the canoes. Ghost-Keeper took a few steps and looked around one of the many tent corners. He grinned from ear to ear, and headed for the riverbank.

"Now what?" Eric asked.

The three of us followed the storyteller. A dozen Cree were lined up along the bank, yelling and waving at three approaching canoes. I saw the chief walking toward all the action, and I don't know why, but he didn't look happy. He pushed a few teenagers out of his way and then barked orders, which people seemed to ignore.

"Stop!" I hissed.

Eric froze in front of me and Anna bumped into my back.

"Someone's coming from downriver," I said.

Anna pushed past me so she could see. "It must be the trading party returning."

"Perfect," I said.

"Why is that perfect?" Anna asked.

Eric laughed. "Because this is a terrific diversion. Everyone will be distracted with the return of the traders down by the water, and we can slip away."

We walked to the teepee and collected our gear. We tried hard to make it look like we were not in a hurry as we walked away from the camp. I felt bad not saying goodbye, but we needed them to think we were just going for a walk. If the chief suspected we had figured out a way home, he might send his men to stop us.

When we were back in the bush and out of sight of the camp, we started hustling.

"I sure hope Rachel and Léon are still at the stones," Anna said, trying to catch her breath.

I slowed down a bit too. "Don't worry," I said, trying to sound confident. "We're all going home together."

Anna offered to carry Eric's backpack for a while, and he accepted. He slipped it off his shoulders and passed it to her without stopping. Ten minutes later, we switched again. I shuffled my backpack off, letting Eric bounce with it through the forest.

My heart wasn't just beating fast because of the quick pace. There was still a chance that we hadn't interpreted the symbols correctly. Or that we had already missed whatever astrological event was supposed to send us home.

The thought of never seeing Sultana again—my Sultana—was unbearable. I already missed my parents, and my bed, and spying on Dr. Murray, and . . .

and everything, really. We had to find Rachel, and we had to get home. The feeling of panic and my desire to leave gave me a fresh burst of energy. I picked up my tired feet and continued slogging toward the ancient stones.

Another five minutes later, Eric blurted, "We made it!" He kept jogging until he was at the centre of the petroform.

Anna followed him and threw her pack on the ground next to his. I examined the shadows around the stones, but it was hard to tell if we had missed the solstice or not.

This was cutting it way too close, I thought.

"Rats!" Anna said. "They are not here!"

Rachel hadn't been anywhere on the path, so she should have been here. But she wasn't.

"RACHEL!" Eric screamed.

I cupped my hands around my mouth and joined him. "RACHEL! IT'S TIME TO GO!"

Silence.

I looked at the sun. Was it at its zenith?

"What should we do?" Anna asked.

Panic was taking a firm hold of me now.

"We're not leaving without her," Eric said.

"I know," I said, "but we have to figure something out."

"Hey, there's Léon," Eric said, pointing toward the south.

I searched for a glimpse of a smaller figure next to him—but he was alone.

We rushed to meet him as he walked toward us.

"Where is she?" I demanded. We didn't have time for polite small talk—we had to find Rachel.

He didn't even bother asking us why we were back at the stones. "She has travelled through zee stones," he said.

"And why would she do that?" Eric challenged.

"We were looking at some of zee symbols on zee stones and . . . and we discovered a way for you all to return home today." I watched a bead of sweat run down Léon's agitated face.

Anna said what we were all thinking. "That does not sound like Rachel."

Léon's eyes darted all over like he was watching a Ping-Pong game. "Rachel wanted me to fetch you . . . to send you through after 'er. Come, you must hurry. The time will run out soon."

"I do not believe you," Anna snapped.

"You're a liar," Eric shouted.

"*Non*," Léon said. "You must get into position now!"

I glanced up at the sun high above us, and my heart sank. We only had a few minutes left to make a decision—leave without Rachel, and hope Léon was telling the truth, or look for Rachel and risk missing our chance altogether.

Léon wiped his sweaty face and tried to compose himself. "Please. You must follow Rachel and go 'ome."

"Sure, sure," Eric said. "You just want to get rid of us three."

This was nuts! We didn't have time for a stupid debate.

And then I had an idea.

"Okay," I said, trying hard to sound friendly. "You're right. We'd better follow Rachel. We were just nervous because we didn't want to abandon her here. That's all."

I hoped I knew what I was doing.

CHAPTER 11

LÉON GAVE US a smile that I knew was phony.

I whispered in Anna's ear, "Count to ten and have a tantrum. After I take care of him, we'll spread out, find Rachel, then meet back here at the stones."

Anna looked at me like I was nuts.

"Okay," I said to Léon, before Anna could argue with me. "Let's do this."

He paused, gave me a suspicious look and said, "I think you should be the first to go." Léon pointed to the centre of the petroform.

Uh-oh! I think he's on to me. I took a few steps, then Anna yelled, "I AM NOT GOING ANYWHERE!"

Léon spun around and stared at Anna.

"You do not 'ave a choice." Léon said. He reached out, like he was going to push Anna into the centre—into the wormhole.

But I was ready.

With every ounce of strength I could muster, I jumped in the air and gave him a vicious karate chop across the back of the neck—just like in the movies. WHACK! Only he didn't collapse onto his face like in the movies. I mean, sure he fell to his knees from the force of the blow, but he wasn't unconscious. He stood up slowly and gave me his creepiest smile yet—a smile that said "now you really made me mad."

Eric said, "Uh-oh!"

"RUN!" I screamed. "Stick to the plan!"

Eric and Anna bolted for the trees on the west side of the petroform. I ran into the woods on the east. Glancing over my shoulder, I saw Léon begin loping after me. I was pretty sure he had lied about Rachel travelling through the wormhole, which meant she had to be around the petroforms somewhere. But where? I figured we had about five minutes to find her before . . . Well, you know.

Zigzagging left and right, I raced around the site, trying to lose Léon while trying to find Rachel at the same time. I ducked behind a tree and peeked around it. I'd lost him. He was nowhere in sight. Maybe my blow to his head had slowed him down after all.

I ran ahead, calling her name as loudly as I dared. "RACHEL!"

We had to bring her home. It wouldn't be right to leave her behind. But if we didn't find her . . . could we risk staying behind? And what if Léon was telling the truth?

"RACHEL!" I heard Anna's voice. "WHERE ARE YOU?"

We were seriously running out of time.

KA-KAWWW! A raven called out somewhere ahead of me.

Come on, Rachel, where are you?

The stupid raven cried out again. KA-KAWWW!

Was that a warning call? Was it trying to tell me something? I tore through the forest in the direction of the eerie bird noise. Branches scratched at my face and arms as I bolted toward the raven.

Rachel! I stopped dead in my tracks. She was lying behind a fallen tree. Her arms and legs were bound with a short length of homemade rope, and she had a leather gag in her mouth.

"SHE'S OVER HERE!" I bellowed, not caring anymore about stupid Léon.

I gently pulled the gag from her mouth. She was

shaking, but still managed to talk. "I was so worried you guys would leave without me," she whispered. "I thought I would be stuck here, with him, forever."

"We wouldn't leave without you, Rach," I assured her.

Eric crashed through the trees. He froze when he saw Rachel, but then moved to help me untie the rope around her arms and legs. Together we assisted her to her feet and got her moving back in the direction of the pillars.

Anna found us halfway. "Where is he?" she said.

"He was chasing me," I said, "but I think I lost him."

"If we're lucky," Eric said, trying to catch his breath, "he tripped on a log and bashed his head."

"And if we are unlucky," Anna said, "he has run back to camp to fetch more men."

"We have to get in that wormhole before they come back," I said.

At the stones, we stuck to the original plan to send Anna and Rachel through first. Anna kept an arm around a still-shaky Rachel to steady her, while Eric and I waited for the shortcut to the future to open up.

"He knew we were going to try to leave today," Rachel said, sounding almost like herself again. "He wanted Anna and you guys to leave, but he wanted me to stay. He said I reminded him of Elyse, his sister."

"Yes," Anna said, "but it is going to be okay now. We will all be home soon."

"What a sneak," Eric said, pacing around the girls. "What a dirty rat."

The four of us waited for the sun to reach its zenith.

A minute passed.

And then another.

"Please work this time," Rachel mumbled. "Please take us home."

Thirty more seconds.

"Did you hear that?" Eric asked.

"Shhh!" Rachel hissed.

This time we all heard it. It started like it had done in the cemetery, when Rachel vanished—with the faint sound of electricity. First a few quiet static snaps, like wires touching a car battery, and then louder charges, like from a lightning strike . . .

And then they were gone. It was like someone took a movie screen and pushed the top and bottom together, while a movie was still playing. The girls collapsed into a single point of light and then vanished.

Eric pumped his fist into the air. "Excellent!"

"Thank goodness," I said. "Now it's our turn."

But before I could step into the centre, where Anna and Rachel had been, two powerful arms yanked me backward. I spun around and stared up into the face of a furious-looking Léon Leblanc.

I glanced beside me for Eric, but he had his own problems. Two young men held his arms and he wasn't going anywhere either.

"Let me go!" I yelled. "We want to leave!"

"Zee chief will decide your fate," Léon snarled.

"That'll take too long, you idiot!" Eric screamed. "Let go of us right now. We're running out of time."

"I would 'ave let you three leave," Léon said. "I only wanted Rachel to stay."

Suddenly we heard a mob of people coming from the direction of the camp. First the pounding of feet reached us, followed by excited talking. The chief and what looked like the rest of the camp had followed us to the pillars. Most of the Cree stayed away from the triangle formed by the three stones. But the chief and several men walked right up to us.

Léon shook his head. "For years I prayed my little sister was well. Elyse was zee only person I truly missed from my old life. Zen when Rachel arrived . . . well, it was like I 'ad my little sister back. I was so 'appy she was sent 'ere . . ."

"No one sent her, you dummy," Eric said. "We told you, everything was an accident. And we're only here to bring the girls back."

"Do not lie to me!" Léon screamed.

That didn't sound good at all.

A large Cree man we didn't recognize stepped forward and spoke to the chief. He must have been away on one of the hunting parties. He had twice as many bear claws and decorations adorning his body as the chief. I blinked and realized: this was the real chief. Raven-Feather may have been a backup chief, or an assistant chief, but this guy was the actual chief.

Barks-Like-An-Otter pushed her way through the small crowd and ran to the large man. He scooped her up with one powerful arm and hugged her close. Barks-Like-An-Otter pointed a finger at Eric, and then at me, and started jabbering in Cree. The man's eyes widened, and he gave her a tight hug before he set her down on the grass again.

Léon began sweating like crazy and tried to get the attention of the men near him. But before he could finish whatever he wanted to say, the chief shouted at the men holding Eric.

They immediately let go of his wrists and backed off.

Léon started to whine, but the chief pushed him away from me. Then the chief grabbed both of my shoulders and held me at arm's length. He stared at me for a few seconds, yanked me close, and gave me a bear hug that squeezed the air from my lungs.

Léon continued complaining in Cree, but no one paid him any attention.

The chief pointed at Barks-Like-An-Otter (she was obviously his daughter) and bobbed his head repeatedly while mumbling to me in Cree. I had no idea what he was saying, but it seemed like he was thanking me. He took three giant strides backward and indicated with his hands that we were free to leave through the stones if we wanted to.

Yes, we wanted to.

I was ecstatic! I could have given everyone there— except Léon, of course—a hug. I was that relieved. But we didn't have a second to spare. We needed to dive into that wormhole before it slammed shut again. I nodded my thanks to the chief, gave everyone a quick goodbye wave and joined Eric in the centre of the pillars.

I glanced at the sky, hoping the sun was still at its max. My legs threatened to collapse under me.

Were we too late?

"Wait!" I heard Eric say. "I think it's . . ."

I turned to face him, but he had already started to vanish. Something pulled and twisted at my body, and then I spiralled down a void until I either blacked out or fell asleep—I'm not really sure which.

"Cody!" a voice said.

"Come on, wake up." A different voice now, with a pleasant German accent. Here we go again, I thought.

"Hey, we made it!" That was definitely Eric.

I turned my head and groaned. "Are we back in Sultana?"

"Yup," Eric said. "And now it's time to tell Bruno the good news."

I finally opened my eyes. Eric, Rachel, and Anna were on their knees, smiling down at me. The sun was still high in the sky, and I guessed it was late afternoon. I sat up and looked around quickly.

Pillars, gravestones, trees, grass—excellent! I smiled. We were in Sultana.

I dug out Bruno's cell phone, turned it on and waited for the time and day to appear.

"What day was it," I said, "when we fell into the wormhole here?"

"Tuesday," Rachel said.

Anna nodded.

"Then we've got a problem," I said. "A big problem. It's Thursday now." I showed everyone the display.

Eric scratched his head. "How the heck are we going to explain where we were for two days?"

"We could be honest," Anna said, "and tell the world what we have experienced."

"Nobody is going to believe us," Rachel said, "except your dad, of course."

We debated our options for a few more minutes, but no one had any new ideas.

Finally, I said, "Why don't I call home and see what's going on?"

"Might as well get it over with," Eric said.

I dialled my house, and after one ring my mom answered.

"Hi, Mom," I said. "It's me. We're back."

"Oh, thank heavens," she cried. "We were all so worried about you kids. Did you find that girl?"

"Uhhm, yes."

"That's tremendous, Cody. Dr. Wassler told us all about it. I'm so proud of you and Eric and Rachel for helping search the forest for her. I just wish you would have called first. Your father is furious. We never imagined you'd get lost too. You can just be thankful the nights are warm."

"Yeah, I am," I mumbled.

"Search parties are still out looking for you," she rambled. "And you know what? They never found a trace. It was like you all just vanished. It was horrible for me and Mrs. Summers. Anyway, Dr. Wassler is right here. Hold on . . ."

A few seconds later, Bruno was on the phone. "I am so very pleased to hear you are back," he said, fighting to control his emotions.

"And we're all happy to be back," I said, assuring him Anna was with me too.

"Thank you again," he said (much louder than he needed to, by the way), "for searching the forest for my daughter when she wandered away from the cemetery and got lost."

I was starting to catch on now, so I said, "You never told anyone about the stones, eh?"

"That is correct. We will drive over to the cemetery now to pick you all up." He laughed awkwardly, and then added, "Be prepared to answer many questions."

My friends had been leaning in, attempting to hear what was happening on the other end of the line.

"What the heck's going on?" Eric whispered.

"Yes," Anna said, "is something wrong?"

I quickly explained what her dad had said on the phone. "So because he didn't tell anyone about the wormhole," I concluded, "we can't either—"

"But why would Papa lie?" Anna interrupted. "We are his proof. The world will now see that he is not crazy. Humans have time-travelled using the petroforms."

"And we can use this as proof," Eric said proudly. He was holding the arrowhead Ghost-Keeper had made for us. "See this little feather he carved onto the side? That's like his signature."

Rachel shook her head. "I agree with Cody. If Anna's dad is keeping quiet about the wormhole, we should too. We have to."

I nodded. "And if he's keeping quiet about the secret of the stones, he must have a very good reason."

"But this will put Sultana in the spotlight forever," Eric said, turning the arrowhead over and over. "Imagine the money tourists would pay to travel back in time."

"Maybe Anna's dad imagined exactly that," Rachel said.

"Huh?" Eric said.

Anna frowned, and then said, "Perhaps Cody and Rachel are both right. My father is a good man. He has spent his life pondering the puzzle of the stones. Now that he has solved the mystery, I do not think he would want to see the petroform exploited, or to see modern man interfering with past civilizations."

Suddenly we could hear people shouting and heading toward us from the direction of the graveyard.

"They'll find us soon," I whispered.

"Okay," Eric said, "here's what happened. Anna wandered off and got lost. Dr. Wassler happened to find us and asked for our help. The three of us (being awesome and helpful kids) ran home, grabbed some gear and headed into the forest to search for her. Right?"

We all nodded.

"Then we got disoriented and became lost our-selves," Eric continued. "But eventually we found Anna near . . . near where?"

"Shoe Lake?" Rachel suggested.

"Perfect," I said. "That's a reasonable distance."

"And then," Eric finished, "we all hiked back here from Shoe Lake."

"Okay," Anna said.

"Nice," I agreed.

"I hope this works," Rachel said.

"Can I still show people the arrowhead?" Eric asked.

CHAPTER 12

"WHY DIDN'T YOU follow your daughter into the forest?" a CBC reporter asked Bruno.

He cleared his throat, and the four of us waited to hear what lie he would tell the media next.

"I . . . I felt it was important for me to remain in the cemetery," he said, "in case Anna should return. Plus, the children assured me that they knew the local trails better than I did."

"But why didn't you go with the kids," another reporter asked, "and help them in the search?"

That question seemed to stump Bruno, and the hall fell silent. Eric rescued him by blurting, "I told him we didn't want him along. He's really old and he would have only slowed us down."

Everyone accepted that and laughed at Eric's cheekiness.

The last three hours are kind of a blur, but I'll try to explain what happened. After being rescued at the cemetery, we were all shuttled over to the community club (that's where we were now). The big hall was the command centre for the police and for the volunteers searching for us. And it was also the gathering place for reporters and TV crews who swarmed Sultana to cover the story of a lost girl and the three kids who were attempting to find her.

Anyway, after the paramedics checked us over, and after the search parties were radioed and told the good news that we were alive, we all had to sit at a long table in front of the media and face a barrage of questions.

The reporters who didn't know about our fake tablet seemed to be impressed with our selfless venture into the Canadian wilderness to rescue a young girl. However, some reporters recognized us. They knew we were the same three kids who had fooled the world with a fake Egyptian artifact weeks earlier. And those reporters asked tricky questions, like the ones they were firing at Bruno. But even if they suspected something weird was going on, I didn't think they could figure out what it was. After all, our story made sense, and we had a world-famous researcher (Dr. Wassler) backing us all the way.

"Okay," the police officer in charge said. "I think these kids have been through enough. Let's end the press conference with that question. And please give the families a week before you contact them for follow-up interviews."

Bruno wiped the sweat from his forehead with a handkerchief and then thanked the police and volunteers again.

"Thank goodness that's over," Eric whispered to me.

"Yeah, for a minute there I thought we were busted."

"The sniffer dogs?" Eric said.

I nodded.

One of the reporters had asked the police why the sniffer dog hadn't picked up our scent when we went after Anna. But before the police could respond, the volunteer dog handler jumped in and explained. He told the reporter that his dog had tracked us in the cemetery and on the trail to Eric's house. But, he explained, the dog was getting old and was probably distracted by all the other smells on the forest trails.

Anyway, the media seemed satisfied with our version of events, and the hall cleared quickly. Bottom line, we were heroes for finding Anna and bringing her back safely. Eric said that was fitting and appropriate (although not entirely true), because we really did bring her back safe and sound. We hadn't gone into the woods, of course, but we did go into a wormhole, on a much more dangerous rescue mission.

"Everything's exactly how we left it," Eric said, staring at the lawn mowers in the graveyard.

"Well, what did you expect?" Rachel asked.

"I'm not sure," he said shrugging.

"Do you think they should have cut the grass for you," Anna suggested, "before they sent the search party to look for you?"

Eric laughed. "I suppose not. But it's kind of weird that we time-travelled through a wormhole and . . . and nothing changed here. And now we're just supposed to carry on mowing the stupid grass and trimming around the stupid graves."

I grabbed a shovel from the wheelbarrow and continued on to the three pillars.

It was the next day now—three days since we

vanished—and everything was almost back to normal. Bruno had to file some police reports at the station in Milner's Corner, leaving Anna to spend the morning with us.

Don't get me wrong, everyone believed our story at the press conference, and he wasn't in any trouble. He was a respected scientist, after all. It's just that the search and rescue efforts to find us cost a ton of money, and I guess everything had to be properly documented.

Anyway, when we arrived at the pillars, I started digging around the base of one of the stones. When I got down a foot I stopped, and we examined the surface.

Anna brushed away the dry earth and said, "Just as you predicted, Cody. More and more of the symbols were buried as the years went by."

"But they're definitely the same," Eric said, getting on his knees and examining the surface. "Hey, wait a minute!"

"What is it?" Rachel asked.

"Look," Eric said. "Look right here, in the corner."

So I did. "Is that . . . what I think it is?" I said.

Eric laughed. "That's exactly what you think it

is. It's a feather. Just like the one Ghost-Keeper scratched on our arrowhead."

"We never noticed it because it's so small," Eric said, "but I bet it was there all along."

Anna scratched her head. "So if Ghost-Keeper wrote those instructions on the pillars, he may also have time-travelled as a teenager."

"Cool!" Eric said.

I got goosebumps on my arms, but said nothing.

"You know," Rachel said, "I'm happy to be back in our Sultana, but if we had to stay with the Cree forever, I don't think it would have been so bad."

I nodded. "You're right about that." I had been thinking the same thing for days. The Cree were super-friendly, they liked to laugh and tell stories, and they took good care of each other. Sure, we had visited them hundreds of years in the past, but in a lot of ways they were just like us. And even if they didn't have computers and other modern stuff, they were happy. "I could have been Ghost-Keeper's assistant storyteller," I added.

"And I could have been the camp chef," Eric said.

"And I would have liked to be a healer," Anna said. "An expert in natural medicines."

"Heck, if they had TVs and pizza, I wouldn't even have bothered coming back with you guys."

"Wouldn't it be neat to go back and visit them some time?" I said.

"Well," Eric said, "that shouldn't be a problem. We know the secret now to go back and visit the Cree. We just have to wait for the right time and stand in the right spot."

"Are you nuts?" Rachel cried. "You can't keep interacting with the past. I thought we settled that already."

"Yes," Anna said, "my father was right. People from the twenty-first century can never use the wormhole again. It must be forgotten."

"We know, we know," Eric said. "We only meant it might be neat to visit them again—like for a holiday. We weren't serious. We were joking."

Rachel mumbled, "Sure, sure."

Anna said, "I suspect you two were only half-joking."

Rachel headed to the edge of the cemetery and began searching the forest floor. "Come on, you guys!" she yelled. "I want to show you something else."

We followed her patiently as she weaved a path around trees and shrubs.

"If we go any farther," Anna cautioned, "we may really get lost."

"Ah ha!" Rachel said, pointing at the ground. "I thought I recognized his name."

I looked down at the grass where a small boulder was half-buried. The rough etching on the exposed surface said:

L. LEBLANC

−1782−

LOST

"I think this might be the very first gravestone in the cemetery," Rachel said.

"I guess his fellow voyageurs assumed he was lost for good," I said.

Eric leaned over and brushed some pine needles from Léon's headstone. "Well, he actually was lost for good, from this world," Eric reminded us.

"The funny thing is," Rachel said, "we found him hundreds of years later, still living happily with the Cree."

I looked at my friends. "Except Léon didn't want to come home," I said, "and we're happy to be home."

Very happy.

AUTHOR
Q & A

Q *In Book One of the Shenanigans series, Cody, Eric, and Rachel create a fake ancient Egyptian tablet to bring much-needed attention to their sleepy town. In Book Two, they stumble upon a real archaeological discovery that has the potential to bring even more fame and attention to Sultana and change their lives forever. How did the kids' experience in the first book influence their actions in the second book?*

A In the first book, Cody, Eric, and Rachel learned the importance of owning up and taking responsibility for one's actions. Specifically, their fake ancient Egyptian tablet created havoc and spun out of control, so they confessed their involvement and faced the consequences. In Book Two, after the kids returned from their time travels to the past, they were presented with an even greater dilemma. If they told the world about the stones, they would be famous and Sultana would remain in the spotlight forever. But because of their recent awareness of consequences, they realized that in spite of the perceived benefits (fame and fortune), past civilizations could suffer greatly from time travellers.

Q *How did you decide to explore the idea of time travel in this book? Are the stone pillars that Cody, Eric, Rachel, and Anna use to travel through time based on real artifacts? And if so, are there people who believe that such artifacts are connected to time travel?*

A I've always been intrigued with the concept of time travel, because if time travel is possible, then any adventure we imagine is also possible. For example, we could go back in time and help build the Great Wall of China. Or we could travel the West Indies with Christopher Columbus. Or we could watch dinosaurs . . . I get inspired just thinking about all the possibilities.

The pillars in *Stones of Time* are loosely based on the great monoliths found scattered across Europe. I'm not sure if any those are arranged in a triangular pattern like those in this book, or if anyone believes those pillars are linked to time travel. That's just the fictional device I used to mark the wormhole.

Q *You could have sent the characters to any time period or any place in the world. Why did you choose to send* them back to the site of their own town, before there ever was a town? What did you want them to see and learn from this experience?

A Yes, they could have travelled back in time anywhere, but I didn't want the kids to be overwhelmed. I thought if they could be grounded in their home town, they would only need to concentrate on the problem of returning to their own time. I also wanted Cody and his friends to experience the Cree culture and to see that people who we think are different are really not different at all.

Q *What would you say to kids who are studying Canadian history in school and finding it boring or hard to connect to?*

A Sure, memorizing dates is kind of dull, but if you can imagine yourself there, in the exciting stories that make up our history, you'd find our past is anything but boring. And don't forget to ask your librarian for middle-grade historical fiction involving the subject/time period you're studying.

Q *What's next for Rachel, Cody, and Eric? Will we see more of Anna and Bruno Wassler in the next book?*

A Cody, Eric, and Rachel have to solve a mystery on their own in Book Three, but Anna and her father will make a reappearance in Book Four.

QUESTIONS for DISCUSSION

1. Do you believe that time travel is possible? Why or why not? If you had the choice to visit either the past or the future, which would you choose and why?

2. How would you describe Anna's character? How would you describe Dr. Bruno Wassler?

3. Cody tells us that the graveyard creeped out him and his friends at first, but then they got used to being there. How would working in a cemetery make you feel? Would you find it peaceful? Sad? Scary? Why?

4. If a stranger approached you and said he found a way to time-travel, would you believe him? What if he had proof? What kind of proof would you need?

5. Cody and Eric race home and quickly gather supplies for their rescue mission. Did they forget to take something you would have taken? Brainstorm a list of things would you want to take with you if you had to travel back in time. But remember, you can only fill two backpacks.

6. If you had a choice and could travel back in time to anywhere, what would you want to see or do?

7. Léon Leblanc, the voyageur, accidentally travelled back in time and decided to stay with the Cree. What do you think of his decision?

8. After spying on the camp where Rachel is held, Cody and Eric hatch a rescue plan. Try and think of a rescue plan that is different from theirs.

9. After successfully escaping and making it home again, Cody and his friends decide they cannot tell anyone that they time-travelled. Do you agree with their decision? Why or why not?

10. Communication is an important theme in this

story. The symbols on the pillars send a message to anyone who can decipher them. When the kids go back in time, they have to learn how to communicate with the Cree, even though they do not speak the same language. Somehow, the characters in the book figure out how to understand things that are completely outside of their normal, everyday experience. Pretend that you have just arrived in a strange place and time, and you have to communicate with the people you meet. How would you do this?

QUESTIONS for
READING COMPREHENSION

1. In the prologue, we see a girl (Anna) lost in a forest. What clues did Anna find to help her figure out where (and when) she was?

2. Why are Cody, Eric, and Rachel cutting the grass in the Sultana cemetery?

3. Dr. Bruno Wassler finds the kids and asks for their help. Why does he have such a hard time explaining what happened? And why do Cody, Eric, and Rachel have a hard time believing him?

4. Based on Cody and Anna's description of the stones, draw a picture of the petroform site.

5. Where was Rachel standing when she vanished? Why is that spot significant?

6. Why can't Bruno go back in time and rescue the girls?

7. If phones don't work in the past, why do Cody and Eric ask Bruno for a phone?

8. What is the name of the astronomical event that will open the wormhole?

9. Why does Bruno tell the boys not to linger in the past? What are the consequences of hanging out with a past civilization?

10. What does Bruno warn the boys about just before they disappear in the wormhole?

11. After Anna finds Cody and Eric, Cody realizes they are actually still in Sultana. What makes him think that?

12. How do the kids lose the Cree trackers that are searching for them?

13. Where does Anna say she is from? Where does she go to school?

14. Why do they decide that Cody should investigate the Cree camp alone? Do you agree with their decision? Why or why not?

15. How does Cody disguise himself when he goes to spy on the Cree?

16. Based on Cody's observations, try to draw a picture or a map of the Cree camp.

17. What clues make Cody think the tall "Native" man is a voyageur?

18. Plan A is to trick the Cree into releasing Rachel using a "talking" tree. What was their back-up scheme—their Plan B?

19. Why does Eric try to change his voice when he talks to Red Hat/Léon Leblanc?

20. Why is Rachel more upset than the others when they learn Léon can actually speak English?

21. What do Eric and Cody do to help the girl who was swimming?

22. What gift does Cody give the chief? Why is the chief so pleased with it? Can you think of anything else Cody could have given him?

23. The chief tells the kids they can go if the stones let them. But the wormhole doesn't seem to work anymore. Why does Cody think the meteor shower won't happen for another month?

24. What does Cody mean when he says "the pillars are like the departure board at an airport"?

25. What is the name of the story Cody makes up to entertain the Cree? Whom are the characters in this story based on?

26. Which band member helps Cody and Eric interpret the symbols on the stone? Who helps Anna come to the same conclusion?

27. What astronomical event do the symbols near the base of the stone describe?

28. What is engraved on the arrowhead given to the boys?

29. When Cody, Eric, and Anna race to the stones to find Rachel, they bump into Léon. He claims that Rachel already left through the wormhole. Why don't they believe him?

30. How does Cody try and overpower Léon? Does it work?

31. Leon wants the kids to stay with him, in the past. What do you think he fears will happen if they travel back to their time?

32. When the real chief arrives at the pillars, Barks-Like-An-Otter says something to him. What do you imagine she said?

33. All four children travel safely back to the present, but as soon as they arrive they have a new problem. What is it? Why does it complicate matters?

34. Who saves Bruno when a reporter stumps him at the press conference? Why are some reporters suspicious of the whole story?

35. Back at the cemetery, Cody digs around one of the pillars. What does he find, and why is it significant?

ABOUT the AUTHOR

ANDREAS OERTEL WAS born in Germany but has lived most of his life in Eastern Manitoba. He now lives with his wife Diane on the beautiful Lee River, near Lac du Bonnet, Manitoba, Canada.

Andreas has degrees from the University of Winnipeg and the British Columbia Institute of Technology, and a lifelong passion for archaeology, ancient civilizations, and writing, especially for young people. In addition to creating fun books for tweens, Andreas enjoys travelling, reading, watching movies, and exploring the great outdoors.

Andreas is the tallest writer in Canada (194 centimetres, or 6 feet 4 inches) and can often be found exploring Manitoba beaches with his trusty metal detector, Lucky.

Visit andreasoertel.com to learn more about Andreas and the Shenanigans books.

Turn the page for a preview of

TrouBle at ImPact Lake

Book Three in the Shenanigans Series

Mysterious strangers are exploring
Sultana's old military base. Can
Cody, Eric, and Rachel discover what
they're up to?

*Coming Fall 2015 from
Wandering Fox Books*

"HEY," ERIC SAID suddenly, "is that a boat?"

I looked around Eric. Up ahead, pulled onto a gravelly beach, was a small overturned fishing boat. It was made of aluminum, about the size of a row boat, and it must have been there for years. Moss and other small plants were actually growing on the bottom, suggesting that the boat hadn't been used in a while.

"Neat," Rachel said, "it looks like someone forgot about it."

"Or died," Eric said, giving the boat a tap with his running shoe.

Rachel took a step back and looked around. "Huh."

Eric laughed. "I don't mean they died right *here*. I mean some old guy, who liked fishing here, might have died in the city. And maybe his relatives didn't even know this boat existed."

"*Or*," I said, "it leaks like crazy and no one wants to get it fixed."

Rachel examined the back of the boat, where an outboard motor might have hung decades ago. She bent over, wiped the grime away, and said, "It doesn't have a name."

Eric snickered. "It's an old fishing boat, Rachel. It's not a cruise ship."

"I know *that*, smarty pants." She stood up and readjusted

the straps on her backpack. "But sometimes people name a boat just for fun."

I nodded. "That's true. Mr. Jelfs has a boat kinda like this one behind his garage. And he has *Stinky* painted on it." I'd never seen him use it, but I always wondered why he'd call it that.

We left the boat-with-no-name and headed back into the forest. I took the lead and found the trail around the lake almost immediately—it was right behind the gravel beach. And *that* was where we encountered every hiker's worst nightmare.

Rachel grabbed my backpack, stopping me dead in my tracks. Up ahead, a big black bear was working his – or her, I suppose—way toward us, eating the wild strawberries that grew along the trail.

The noise Eric had heard earlier made sense now. The bear hadn't seen us yet, but he was heading right for us. In about a minute he would be sniffing our feet with his huge muzzle. My legs seemed glued to the ground, but I knew we had to do something.

I turned my head and as quietly as I could I said, "Back up . . . slowly."

We each took several paces backward.

SNAP!

Eric or Rachel must have stepped on a fallen branch. *Nuts!*

The bear's shaggy head shot up—his alert ears listened for signs of danger like tiny satellite dishes. Seconds passed by, and I thought he was going to go back to eating. But then his beady eyes settled on me, and I knew for certain we were in big trouble.

Now what? I thought.

The what-to-do advice we had always heard about bear encounters was never the same. Sometimes we were told to curl up into a ball and play dead, while other experts said to climb a tree or to yell and make lots of noise. In our case, I didn't think he'd be fooled by us lying down on the ground. That would only make it easier for the bear to get his snack—three tasty kids. And would yelling really discourage an animal as large as a bear? I sure doubted it. I briefly considered climbing a tree, but there was no way all three of us could scramble up a tree fast enough to outrun the bear. So forget that.

The bear took a few cautious steps forward.

I matched him with three even more cautious steps backwards.

Think, Cody. You have to do something.

The bear snorted, sending a wave of goosebumps up my arms.

I took a few more steps backward, never taking my eyes off the approaching bear. I didn't dare turn around to see where my friends were, but I sensed they were retreating too.

Maybe we could use the boat to escape, I thought. But there was no way we could drag it to the water *and* launch it successfully without being mauled first.

The bear waved his enormous head back and forth menacingly.

"Cody, the boat," Rachel whispered. "We could use the boat."

"I don't think we have time," I said quietly. "Plus, it might not even float."

"No!" she said. "I mean, we could hide *under* it—it's metal. We might be safe there."

I took another step back. "Good thinking." There were no other options available to us. We had to seek shelter somewhere, and the old boat was our best bet.

"Just keep walking backwards," I said, "slowly. If he starts to run . . . then we'll turn and—"

"RUN!" Rachel screamed. "RUN !"

The last thing I saw before I spun around was the bear

charging toward us. Eric was already out of sight. Rachel was three paces ahead of me, tearing back to the boat. We both broke onto the beach to find Eric struggling to lift one side of the vessel.

Panting from exertion, Rachel and I grabbed the edge of the boat on either side of Eric. We wrestled and strained to raise it, but the stupid thing would barely budge. Weeds and small trees had latched onto the boat over the years and we fought against them to rip the side free. Suddenly the boat became a lot lighter, and we were able to lift it enough to get beneath it.

"Quick, Rachel," I ordered. "Get under!"

She dove in the gap between the front of the boat and the first row of seats.

At the same time I heard the bear crashing through the undergrowth behind me.

"Go! Go! Go!" Eric screamed.

I tried to wedge myself in the rear of the boat, but I forgot I was wearing the bulky backpack. It got caught on the gunwale, leaving me half under the boat and half exposed.

"Hurry!" Eric cried. "He's getting closer!"

I scrambled to free my bag and get back under the boat. I rolled onto my back and used my legs to keep the boat raised so that Eric could join us. "I got it!" I bellowed. "Get under!"

I saw the bear storming toward us as Eric fell to his knees and rolled under the mid-section of the boat. When Eric was safely under, I bent my knees and let the weight of the boat seal us in.

SLAM!

The bear thumped into the boat a second later. The boat shuddered violently but stayed put.

"Man, was that close!" I heard Eric say in the dark. His voice echoed eerily under our aluminum shelter.

I groped in the dark for my flashlight and flicked it on. "Is everyone okay?" I asked, waving the beam around.

Rachel said, "Yeah," but her voice was pretty shaky.

"I think I have to pee," Eric said, "but I'm all right."

Through the gaps under the boat's seats, I could see Eric and Rachel clearly. The deeper shape of the bow gave Rachel a lot more room at her end. She was leaning on one elbow, but she had enough space to crawl on her knees. Eric and I, on the other hand, were wedged in pretty tightly.

Outside we heard the bear snorting and grunting in frustration.

BAM!

The bear slammed a giant paw on the boat. I looked above me at the ceiling—which was actually the floor of the boat—and saw a dinner-plate-sized dent appear.

BAM! BAM! BAM!

The noise under the aluminum was deafening.

"Leave us alone!" Rachel yelled. "Go away!"

For a minute, I thought that would work. But then, without warning, the entire boat shifted a few inches. Light spilled from outside and I caught a flash of black fur—lots of black fur.

"Oh, no!" Eric said. "He's trying to do what he saw us do. He's trying to flip the boat!"

Wandering Fox Books

*Contemporary Canadian classics reimagined
for today's young readers*

WANDERING FOX BOOKS is an imprint of Heritage House Publishing, catering to young readers ages eight to sixteen. Wandering Fox titles are timeless Canadian stories by bestselling, award-winning authors who count kids, parents, librarians, and educators among their loyal fans. The name Wandering Fox encompasses the curiosity, mischief, and adventure of young readers on the journey to adulthood.

All books are suitable for classroom use and come with discussion and/or comprehension questions and author interviews.

For more information, or to order books in the series, see wanderingfoxbooks.com, heritagehouse.ca, or hgdistribution.com.

The SHENANIGANS SERIES
Book One

HiSTORY
in the
FAKiNG

ANDREAS OERTEL